MEND THE FLESH

THE PHOENIX SERIES - BOOK THREE

SARAH ROCKWOOD

COME CLOSER

Come closer. The story doesn't end on the page.

Want early access to new releases, behind-the-scenes world building, and occasional letters from my strange and unusual world?

You'll also be the first to know when new episodes of my podcast, *We Make Art*, go live—conversations and reflections for creatives who want to live wide awake.

Sign up and join me on this adventure:

https://sarahrockwood.com/mailing-list/

1

"**W**here are my blades?"

Royal was sitting on a low stool in the yellow sand of his desert hideaway. He rose stiffly to his feet.

"Why are you out of bed, girl?"

"Don't call me 'girl,' it's demeaning," I approached him. "Where are my blades?"

Royal let out a sound of acquiescence.

"I put it somewhere safe."

We were standing almost toe to toe now, like two bedraggled vultures who were both picked clean. Royal metaphorically and me physically. Okay, and emotionally.

"You don't look so good, honey. You need to get back inside. The sun will tear you up with you so raw."

"Take me to my blades."

"Blade. I found one blade," he grunted. "And it's inside, so you might as well head back in there."

I turned on my bony heel and shuffled back into the adobe dwelling. It had been two full days since I'd awoken in this home, raw and burnt down to the bone. How am I still alive, you ask? Well, apparently this is what my people do. Every once in a while if we get very, very stressed we burst into flames. Our wings, our flesh, everything, burning down to bone and sinew, culminating in a giant blast of power. And God help whoever is standing close by.

I don't know what happened to those people. I was locked in a battle for my life when I burned. Mhyr, my boyfriend's crazy ex, had an arm wrapped around my throat and was trying to drain me of my power. Archer, my boyfriend, Mhyr's ex, you get the idea, and about three hundred minions were trying to save me. Unfortunately, Mhyr had surrounded us with an impenetrable dome of power so they couldn't get in. As Mhyr had pulled on my power, my body had freaked out and this ability to regenerate, burst into flames, that I hadn't known about, took over. It scared the crap out of me. I was sure I would die. Archer was sure, too. I could see him on the other side of the dome screaming my name, tears running down his face. So I had burst into flames and woken up here, alone.

Well, not alone, Royal was here. Royal, another of my kind, not my father, even though he sure tried to act like it, was at my bedside. When I had finally given into the burning, and my power had blasted the dome free and shot out across the land, Royal heard my call. I thought I was the only one of our kind, so you can imagine my surprise when I woke up to a grizzled old man with big multi-coloured wings staring down at me. Picture Kris Kristofferson dressed as an angel for Halloween, that's Royal.

"Where is it?" I demanded.

We were now inside, though in this case inside was a relative term. There were no doors in the doorways or glass in the windows; Royal's home was an adobe hut comprising arched ceiling rooms that connected to each other by breezy passages. Despite the heat of the sun outside, inside was cool and shady. Night got cold though, so the primary rooms and sleeping areas had fire pits.

"I put it in the kitchen," he said mildly as he crossed to the cooking area, his fading wings dragging ever so slightly on the floor. "Seemed the best place for something that sharp." On the kitchen counter was my untouched bowl of porridge. Royal glanced at it. "You need to eat."

"I'm not hungry."

"Yes, you are." He bent down to open a cabinet while he talked. "But it hurts your gut; I get it. But if you don't eat, you won't regenerate. And if you don't regenerate, you can't go home to whoever gave you this."

He placed the blade next to my cold porridge.

It was the short sword Archer had given me long before my Banishment, the beautiful blade that had called to me in my weapons room in what seemed like a lifetime ago. I stepped up to the counter and moved to touch the hilt, then hesitated. My raw, sinewy fingers held inches above it. I was sure that if I touched the blade, it would call to Archer. Archer. He was probably losing his mind looking for me. Or he assumed I was dead. And right now he'd be right. Sort of. I looked dead. I looked like I had been rotting in a coffin for months and then changed my mind and started walking around again. I was literally bone, sinew and the odd bit of flesh. I had no hair, no lips, half an eyelid on one eye and, although a thin layer of tissue had grown over my chest cavity, in the light you could see my lungs.

I looked like a walking horror movie. I didn't want Archer to see me like this. I didn't want anyone to see me like this. I tolerated Royal's eyes on me because he'd been through this before and as much as it pissed me off; I needed help. My arms were too stiff to wrap myself up in the light sheets I wore; Royal did that. He also cleaned the last of the dead burnt flesh off my exposed spine and changed the damp sponge I'd had to wear over my eyes those first few days. I couldn't get better without him. I gingerly sat on a stool and began eating my cold porridge.

"Please put that away," I swallowed. It hurt. I got another spoonful. "Thank you. For everything." A tear rolled from my naked eyeball, the salt stung as it travelled down my cheek.

"It's my pleasure," Royal mumbled. Then he picked up the sword. "I'll put this in your room." As he walked past, he placed a hand ever so lightly on my shoulder. "You'll get better real soon, honey." And then he left me to my porridge.

2

———

The days are long in the desert; especially when you have no books or music or television. It doesn't seem to bother Travellers, but I grew up in the human world, and in the human world there's a lot of good tv. I tried talking to Royal, but he preferred to spend the day outside sunning himself on a rock, only coming in occasionally to cook me some porridge or go to the bathroom. The only time we spent together was at night.

After dinner, when the sun was down, he would build fires in all the rooms and then we'd sit together in the living room. Him deep in a beanbag chair and me sitting painfully upright on a straight-back chair that provided enough support for the skeletal remains on my wings. Tonight was the third night of this routine and I longed for conversation as I watched Royal stare at the flames.

"Any adventures you'd like to share?" I asked.

"Hmm?"

"Adventures. You must have a few," I pressed.

"Not really."

"Right." This was going well. "Any bird-person wisdom you'd like to impart to me?"

He turned from the flame and looked at me, the light blue of his eyes seemed to spark in the light.

"Bird-people? Is that what you think we are?"

There was an edge to his voice that I hadn't heard before. I'd struck a nerve. Which was fine with me because sitting here in silence was making me crazy. If having an argument with him was the only way to get him to talk, then so be it.

"I don't know what we are. Until a few days ago, I thought I was the only bird-person around. I meet you and think 'fantastic, now I can learn who we are,' but you don't seem to want to tell me. So until I know different, I'm going with bird-people."

"Bird is their word. Not ours."

"Who are 'they?'"

"Everyone else."

"Okay." Ah, that familiar Traveller crypticness, how I'd missed you. "So what's our word?"

"I'm Royal, and you're Phoenix. And that's all we need."

"So we don't have a name for our species like the Sirens or the Minions do?"

"Nope, don't need one."

"Why not?"

"Because until a few days ago, honey, I was sure I was the only one of whatever we are. And I was fine with Royal."

"Really? You've never met another of our kind?"

"Nope."

"Then..." I paused, "then how did you know to come help me?"

Royal sighed heavily and with a few flaps of his wings

was standing. He moved towards the fire and added another log. I stayed silent, waiting.

"Well, because that explosion of power you let off, and the scream that came with it, they felt just like it did when it happened to me. I'm sitting outside on my rock and suddenly this ripping scream goes through me and every feather in my wings stands on end. I got this image of you, this burnt out thing lying in the dirt, and my heart knew where you were and what had happened to you. So I Travelled to you. Brought you back here." He turned to me, a rough smile on his lips. "Don't go thanking me again. You've done enough of that." He went back to his seat. "And I know you'd do the same thing for me."

"I would."

"I know, honey, you're good people. Good bird-people," he winked.

"Oh, please don't make me laugh." I tried to relax into the shaking of my ribs. "It hurts."

"You're getting better though, more meat on you today."

"Yeah, a bit."

We sat in companionable silence for a few minutes.

"So how many times has this," I gestured at myself, "happened to you?"

"Twice."

"Seriously?" If I'd had eyebrows or even eyelids, they would have shot up. "You've been through this twice?"

"Yep, a long time ago now."

"How did it happen?"

"Well, the first time was sticky."

I waited in the firelight. How many times had I sat round a fire with a fellow Traveller and learned their secrets? Sid had told me my life story by a fire like this. I heard about the tearing of my wings as red and gold flames danced in the reflection of his eyes.

And then there were those hours with Benyst, sat there with stew and beer and quiet companionship. I wondered what they were both doing now. I had freed Sid from the City of Caves. And Benyst had gone back to Noiryn, I'd made sure of that. Sigh. Why did I have to hit on him? He had Noiryn; I had Archer, and yet when I was on top of Benyst, not on top of him, on top of him, we'd fallen after Travelling, my body had made the move. That mistake felt so long ago. In human terms, it was only maybe a week ago. In Travellers' terms? Well, they, sorry, we, seem to see everything on a single continuum. It gets a bit confusing.

"I had decided to go exploring..." Royal began. "I did a lot of exploring when I was younger. I couldn't stay in one place for too long. Sure I had this place, and I loved it here then as much as I do now, but I just needed to fill my eyes with unknown things. I'd just got back from some time in the Grand Canyon, exploring and riding the rapids, and the sandy landscape back here just seemed too familiar. So I jumped into the air and let Time take me. When I'd spun out of the Time Tunnel, I flew over..."

"Wait!" I interrupted. He glared at me. "Sorry, very sorry, it's just, well, we can fly through the Time Tunnels? And be in the air when we come out?"

"Of course we can." He gave me a weird look. "How have you been doing it?"

"Well, I just kind of get dragged along."

He sighed.

"All right, when you're stronger, we'll work on that."

"Thank you."

"Now, if I may continue?"

"Please."

"So I was in the air after the Time Tunnel and I come out to see this massive mountain range below me. Everywhere I looked there were mountains, but green, not snowy white like you usually see. And the air was warm and moist. It was easy to catch a headwind and glide. I did that for a while above the scene, just taking in the mountains. There were no humans around, which made exploring easier, but I knew to always keep an eye out for the big animals."

"Why? I thought they couldn't see us?"

"Who told you that?"

"A friend, they said they could sometimes feel our presence, but it's hard for them to see us."

"Well, your friend is wrong. The bigger the animal, the better it can spot you. And the further back in time you go, the easier they can spot you. Take it from me, don't go trying to see the dinosaurs, you'll be attacked before you can get your feet on the ground. Look at this."

He sat forward and pulled up his shirt, exposing the right side of his body. There were three long ragged gashes, healed over and shiny, they stretched from his armpit down his body and around to his low back.

"Holy crap!"

"Yep, nearly ripped me in half. I managed to get out of there and back home before I bled out."

"I didn't know we could be injured like that."

"Of course we can!" Royal pulled his shirt down. "You cut a minion's head off, and you still think we can't be injured!" he laughed. "Bird, you've got a lot of learning to do."

Yes, I'd cut off a minion's head. Those who feared him called him Greldrom, me, I called him Big G. He was a tyrant and sadist and generally a horrible being, and I'd killed him. At the time I thought he was responsible for the Bounty on my life, but he wasn't, he was just trying to capture me so he could claim the reward. I didn't feel bad about killing him. I'd thought long and hard about it those first few days I laid on my bed here in Royal's home. Greldrom needed to die. So I killed him. I could live with that and still sleep at night. Which honestly scared me more than the actual killing.

Even though I wasn't human, I still wanted to keep my humanity.

"Right, I just thought when we were outside our world we were safe."

"Phoenix, you've got a lot more to learn."

"I know," I looked down at my sinewy fingers; they looked like shrivelled pepperoni in the firelight. I shuddered, sliding my hands into the folds of my robes. "Sorry, I'll stop interrupting. You were gliding over the mountains?"

Royal had watched my brief finger moment but said nothing. Then with a great shuddering sigh he began his tale.

3

"I was gliding around and keeping an eye out for anything big. The coast looked clear, so I made my way to the ground.

I was doing it in wide circles, only a few flaps here and there, just slowly floating my way down. The sun was behind me, and I could see my shadow on the ground. The outline of my wings, the shape of my body, it was kind of hypnotic, and I lost myself in the graceful swirl of me and my shadow.

I was about halfway down when a black shape flitted across the ground below me. At first I thought it was some big mammal down there waiting to pounce on me, so I widened my circle and stopped my descent. But as I circled, clouds closed in behind me, blocking the sun and destroying my shadow for a moment. When the clouds moved, I could make out my shadow below, but it wasn't alone. A little ways away was another shadow, a gigantic shadow, pacing me.

The shadow that followed me was huge, the wingspan easily double my own and the body of the bird, it had to be a bird, twice my size. It was hunting me. I knew it in my bones. If I didn't get out of there quick, I'd be a meal for this monstrous thing.

I had to get back to the portal. You know about portals, right?" He paused and looked at me.

"Yes, please continue," I answered in a hushed tone.

"Had to ask. Right, we can fly through the tunnels and find portals in the air, but you still got to find a portal in the first place. And the portal I needed was up much higher than where I was. So I went into a dive, hoping to draw the bird out and then lose it on the rise. I figured anything that big would have a hard time making altitude quickly. So I took a deep breath and moved to dive.

The bird was on to me though, and much closer than I had realised. I went into the dive and looked back over my shoulder to see if the bird was following. It was enormous. Just bloody huge. The body of the bird was taller than me and twice as wide. It had these thick stubby legs with giant clawed feet, and when I turned to look at it, it dropped into attack mode. It stretched its wings back and stuck out its talons. It was dropping fast, and it was ready to catch me.

I had no time to think; I went on instinct. I pulled out of the drop and flapped my wings; I think I was trying to get out of the way of the bird, but I'd underestimated its wing-span. I moved left and the bird's wing struck me. It was like being hit by a feather-covered tree. It knocked the wind out of me, and I struggled to breathe as I dropped like a stone to the ground.

As I tumbled, I felt the great bird's talons pierce the flesh of my arm as it caught my bicep. It let out a sharp cry, sure it had caught me. But we were too close to the ground for the big guy to stop itself and we crashed through the trees, tangled together. I do not understand how I got my lungs working again, but I did and it brought the sense back to me. As we crashed through the trees, I reached up with my free hand and drove my fist into the belly of the beast. I knew the punch alone wouldn't hurt the bird. So I grabbed onto the short feathers that covered its gut and pulled myself in closer. I heard a tearing sound as I did this and looked down to see the flesh of my caught arm splayed open. I ignored that as best I could and called on my power. A blast of white lightning shot from heart down my arm and into the bird.

It screamed and released me just as we hit the ground. The body of the bird cushioned my fall, and I tried to make my escape. I ran for it, but I was getting weak from blood loss, and I stumbled. That quick stumble was enough time for the bird to right itself and start after me. I knew I had no other choice but to stand and fight the fucking thing.

I looked around for a weapon, and all I could see was a big rock. There was no time to pull down a branch or fashion something sharp. So I picked up that rock with my good arm, charged it with power until it glowed bright blue, then braced myself for the attack.

The bird came at me hard, but I was ready. I went with the impact and held on to the bird's torso. I was too close to its body to be batted by its wings, but it still had that massive beak and it started pecking at my head and shoulders. I crawled up the body of the beast, all the while its beak pecking at me. I buried my head in the bird's neck to protect myself, and then I started pounding on its skull with my rock. Just pounding as hard as I could. It screamed and ripped a long gash down my back with its beak. It was running in circles now, trying to throw me off, but I knew if it did I would be bird seed, so I kept bashing that rock into its skull and it kept running.

My injured arm was going numb and flashes of blackness were coming closer together; I didn't have much time left; I was sure I was going to die. And I swear, as soon as that hit me, the moment I knew this would be my last fight, this warm pulse grew in my belly. At first I thought it was the warmth of death coming for me, but the warmth turned to hot, burning hot, and then it moved through my limbs. It ran down my arms and legs, the rock in my hand freaking melted. Without thinking, almost like I was in slow motion, I reached up and smeared it across the bird's cheek.

It screamed a horrible sound, just freaking horrible. It was as the bird's scream crested that the heat in me doubled and light blue flames erupted from my torso. The bird panicked then and, as the flames moved down my arms and legs, it took to the sky.

It was almost impossible for the beast; big wings are hard to flap so low to the ground, but it was now as close to death as I was. We rocked and bucked as we ascended, all the while the magnificent bird is trying to throw me off. When we reached the sky, warm winds fanned my flames and soon the bird and I were both covered in blue fire. I could smell our feathers burning. The heat inside me was unbearable; I pulled my head from the bird's neck and looked at my body. My clothes had burned away and under the blue flames, blisters covered my skin. I looked like I was cooking from the inside out.

The bird knew we were going to die, and with a last burst of energy, it flapped higher and then went quick into a spiral dive, trying to throw me. The ground coming closer, and I could feel the heat inside me ready to blow. So I let go. I let go of everything.

The last thing I remembered was a bright flash of blue and then nothing."

Royal stared into the fire.

"Then what happened?" I whispered.

"I woke up here."

"Seriously?"

"Well, not right here, just over the hill where the portal is. My best guess is that when I went boom, the bird was blown off and I had the good fortune to fall directly through the portal."

"But you must have been a skeleton when you landed?"

"Pretty much. Still had a bit of meat on me though, woke up to two buzzards picking at me."

"That's gross."

"It was," Royal laughed.

"But how did you get back here? I could barely move those first few days. And how did you take care of yourself?"

"Oh, I had help."

"You did?" He was silent. "Who?"

"Cheryl." He stared at the fire.

"Who's Cheryl?"

"My wife."

He offered no further information, and since Cheryl wasn't living here now, I didn't press it. We sat in silence for a few more minutes.

"And the second time?" I asked.

"Huh?" Royal seemed to come back from somewhere far away.

"The second time you burned, what happened then?"

"Oh, that." He took a swig of his drink and placed the empty cup on the floor. "Well, Cheryl died."

Then he stood up and walked out into the moonlight.

4

———

I watched him go. I didn't try to stop him. Some pains are private, and no matter how often you talk about them or how much time has passed, they never go away. The death of Royal's wife was one of those things. But it also got me thinking, how did he get a wife? Why didn't the role of wife have some strange Traveller name or something? Royal, despite his wings, felt the most human of any Traveller I'd met. Maybe he'd spent a lot of time with humans and picked up some stuff.

I threw a few more logs on the fire so it would still be burning when Royal returned. He didn't need the light to guide him; he knew this land like the back of his hand, but the light of the fire would be welcoming.

My room had two large openings, which Royal affectionately called windows, but without glass, they were just enormous holes in the wall. Sure they had shutters, but thin slats of wood would not stop any desert creepy-crawlies from getting inside. The shutters were open, and moonlight poured through making lighting some candles unnecessary. There was a simple bed up against the back wall just outside the circle of light, and a door beside it led to a bathroom and closet. The best feature of the room was the bathtub. It was a clawfoot number, large enough for me and my wings, and sat directly in the circle of moonlight that spilt through the window.

I turned on the single tap, cold water. If you wanted hot, you had to heat it yourself. As the tub filled, I went over to the full-length mirror Royal had propped against one wall and began the delicate process of unwrapping myself. I went through this every night, and although I could see some progress in my condition, it still took effort not to gag at my reflection.

I had more flesh now, which was great, but sometimes the wrappings stuck to my new raw patches, which meant a slow wiggle-tear process to release them. A thin layer of new flesh covered my skull. I had eyelids now, and you couldn't see the food in my mouth when I chewed. Royal was thrilled about that. My ribcage was thickening up, just a faint shadow of my lungs and heart remained. And my arms and legs were starting to flesh out. Little strips of beef carpaccio stretched from shoulder to elbow and hip to knee. But nothing had skin on it; I guess that would come later. I looked like a moving anatomical diagram designed to display the muscular system. It was a vast improvement from where I'd started, but the raw flesh made me look more disgusting than when I was just bone and burned bits of skin. Yep, I looked gross, horror movie gross.

My wings were still nothing but twigs. They had made no progress at all. I flexed the twiggy bones in the mirror; they moved like rusty hinges.

"Oil can," I mumbled to the darkness.

The tub was just about full, so I began focusing my power to warm it. It didn't take much to heat the water, but I was still fragile, and most of my energy was going to healing. I took a deep breath and let it out slowly. I reached deep into myself and called forth my power. I could see it in my belly, dark and cold, a tiny flame working so hard against the darkness. I called to it, coaxed it forward, and soon it was a warm glow I could hold in my hands. The orb of power pulsated between my palms. Not the tremendous blast of power I had once created, but stronger than the day before. I plunged my hands into the water, and the ball of energy spread out into the liquid. Soon little trails of steam floated from the surface in the cool desert night. I turned off the tap and gently stepped into the water.

The water was the perfect temperature, but my limbs were still stiff and raw; it took a lot of deep breaths to step into the tub. My feet felt strange on its ceramic bottom. I felt each toe as it touched the hard surface; like drumming your fingernails on a tabletop. There wasn't enough flesh on my feet to give me traction, so I gripped the sides of the tub hard to keep from completely falling into the water. I'd learned from my previous attempts at bathing and already had fluffy towels draped over the sides of the tub for my hands to hold as I braced myself. Much like my feet, raw tendon fingers couldn't do much against the smooth ceramic. Without the towels for gripping, I'd be flat on my ass and in a lot of pain. Royal had already had to rescue me twice. Being picked up off the floor feels way more embarrassing when you have no skin. So with beef jerky legs and sinewy hands, I slowly lowered myself into the water. My nerves were raw, literally and figuratively, and everywhere the water touched sang out.

Finally submerged, I sat back against the tub and let myself relax. Royal said the baths would help keep the new flesh soft, and he was right, but it was an exercise in perseverance to look at my broken body as I did it. I was grateful the moonlight reflected off the surface enough to hide the raw flesh from my eyes. I feared the upcoming days of no moon; how would I keep from looking at my strange body then?

My wing stubs, as I affectionately called them since they'd been cut down in size, wiggled tentatively in the water. It was the first time they'd moved on their own since the Burning and I sat bolt upright, sloshing water over the sides of the tub.

"Holy crap!" I exclaimed. "Are you guys back?"

In response to my question, the wings wiggled again.

Yes, my wings answer questions, and yes, my wings are a part of my body, and yes, that makes no sense. But we'd spent so long apart that they had developed an energy of their own. When we joined forces again, they kept some of that power. It was like having symbiotic twins attached to your back. We shared everything, but they still had an element of autonomy.

My wings wiggled again, but the movement was less smooth this time, jerky and a little stiff.

"Right, back in the water."

I slipped back into the water, going deep enough for it to brush my chin. I held myself away from the ceramic, so the wings could get more movement if they so desired. And desire they did.

The wings opened and closed, slowly, like we were soaring amongst the clouds. It felt so good to experience that sensation again. I could almost feel their full glory, and I smiled, genuinely smiled, from my heart, for the first time since the Burning. With the moonlight pouring down on me, I closed my eyes and stretched out in the water, remembering the feeling of flight.

With my eyes closed, they transported me. Like a grainy home movie being played on a sheet in the backyard, the images of our flight played out in my mind. We were soaring through the Void. The land was grey and undulating below us; the ice cold rivers were black lines cutting through the soft rises of the earth. Everywhere I looked the sky was grey, one uniform shade of grey. Distance, Time, they had no meaning here.

I was in love. In love with my home world, with its stark beauty. Its ability to disturb and embrace me. This was home, not my comfortable house in the forest; this was my place of origin, my homeland. This was where I grew my power. This was my land, and it called to me just as my wings did. It called to me through Space and Time as I lay in my bath with my wing stubs wiggling, and through the vision told me I was never alone. I would always have the Void.

The vision broke, and I found myself standing in the bathtub, my wings calm at my back and the light from the moon fading from my flesh. I could feel my feet against the tub; they seemed fuller, more secure. I looked down at myself and saw a shiny fresh layer of muscle over my bones. I smiled, and it didn't hurt. I touched my face and realised not only were my fingers more whole, but my lips were fuller, they covered all of my teeth. I let my hands fall to my side and took a deep breath.

I stepped out of the tub, no need to grip the sides, and walked to the mirror. In the fading light of the moon, I turned my back to see my wings. Though still only bones and bits of muscle, they had grown. A new bone protruded from the end of each wing.

5

———

The next morning I wrapped my newly formed muscles and sinew slowly, examining the new bits of meat that now clung to my bones as I draped myself in a sand-coloured fabric.

I had more flesh on the soles of my feet, which was awesome. Maybe now I could venture out of the house during the day. Even with shoes on, the scorching desert sand felt like hell on my bony feet. I wrapped my wings last; they were the fiddliest part of the process and required a lot of time in the mirror. Even though my body was healing, it was still hard to look at my raw form in the glass. Being fully covered made doing my wings more bearable. Another plus from last night's moon bath was more flesh on my fingers; they almost moved normally. Maybe one day they can handle an actual button! What can I say, I'm a dreamer.

Wings wrapped, I picked my gloves up off the nightstand and tucked them into a swirl of cloth. Unless I went outside, I wanted my hands free.

The last step of the entire wrapping process was the headpiece. Royal and I had experimented with a bunch of different wrapping techniques, most of which left me looking like the invisible man. I finally had gotten so frustrated that I ripped the entire thing off, which hurt a lot and I regretted instantly. Ever had a chapped lip split open? Imagine that all over your face.

We settled on a loose hood that wrapped around my neck and could be pulled up and over to cover my face. Royal didn't seem very squeamish about how I looked, and I couldn't see my face as I went about my day, so I left the hood down, mostly.

Standing in front of the mirror in my full fabric glory, I sighed. I had come a long way; I was healing, but even wrapped my frailty was clear. There was no meat to me; I was ultimately still a skeleton, now a fashionably clothed skeleton, but a skeleton all the same. And my face, my terrible face. High cheekbones look great when you've got skin, but when you are strips of bacon, they look aggressive. It was super depressing. I pulled up my hood and slipped on the gloves, then went to see what Royal was up to.

Royal was up to the usual, making me a giant breakfast and girding his loins for the inevitable battle to make me eat it.

"Morning," he said as he placed a large bowl of oatmeal and three fried eggs on the counter.

"Good morning," I mumbled as I sat down and grabbed my spoon. I tucked into the oatmeal without argument.

"Hey, are you okay?" Royal stood before me, his hands resting on the counter, his bright blue eyes searching mine. I didn't have the energy to lie."Not really," I took a bite of egg. "I thought I'd made actual progress last night, but this morning I look like just another skeleton." I paused, stuffed more egg in my mouth. "I have more meat on my feet, so that's something."

"You will get better," he said softly.

"I know," I smiled at him, my new lips stretching slightly. "I honestly do know that. Some days are just easier than others." I ate another mouthful of oatmeal. Royal smiled.

"Well, if a bad day makes you eat, then I guess I'm good with it."

"So what's the plan for the day?" I asked with my mouth full. A piece of egg fell out.

"Hilarious," he tossed me a napkin. "I'll be preparing the Moon Circle for you."

"Moon Circle?"

"Yep, Moon Circle. With the full moon coming, you need maximum exposure. I build a sacred circle out in the desert and you bathe there as the moon hits its zenith."

"Outside? Like in the open desert?"

"Yep."

"Like, where the animals are?"

"They won't come near, don't you worry."

"How do you know that?"

"Well, for one, all the power you'll be throwing off will scare the crap out of them, and two, I'll be putting up a big circle of protection."

"Makes sense."

"It does," Royal wiped the surrounding countertop where a few specks of oatmeal and egg had formed a ring around my bowl. "You need to do two things today."

"And they are?"

"You need to eat like a horse and rest like a sloth."

"A sloth?" I giggled.

"Yeah, a sloth, they're very restful."

"Oh, I know, it's just not the animal I thought you'd use."

"Can you name me one that does less than a sloth?" he

asked. The corner of his mouth twitched. I'd learned over the last few days that this was Royal being playful.

"Hmm, snail?"

"Nope, they may be slow, but they aren't lazy."

"Sloths are lazy?"

"Have you ever met a sloth?"

"Can't say that I have."

"Well, I've known a few in my time, and they were lazy bastards."

I laughed a little too hard and felt something rip at the corner of my mouth. My hand shot to my lip and came away with blood. "Shit!"

"Don't panic." Royal came around the counter with a clean cloth in his hand. "Hold still." He put one hand gently behind my head and pressed the cloth to my lip. "Don't talk. Just hold still for a few minutes and it'll pass. You've just got to be more careful until this is all healed up."

"Mmm mmm," I mumbled through my closed mouth.

"Don't talk. Just relax."

I took a deep breath in through my nose and let it out as best I could through the side of my mouth to which Royal wasn't pressing cloth. I could feel tears coming. Since my burning, their salt felt like acid against my skin, so I tried a few more deep breaths to keep them at bay.

"Let them out, Phoenix," Royal whispered, "you've got to let it all out."

I looked into Royal's bright blue eyes, framed in wrinkles and holding the weight of many, many years. We were strangers, yet we were kin. He was the only one of our kind I had ever known. There was trust there: an unspoken bond of pain and longing. The skeletal remains of my wings twitched. They wanted to trust him too. And I trusted them.

So we all trusted each other. I took a deep breath and let the tears go.

"Good girl," Royal whispered as he took the cloth from my mouth and used a clean edge to catch the tears before they could get too far along my cheeks. His movements were so caring, paternal, unconditional, and with another deep breath I felt my boney frame soften and the tiny flame of power inside me burn a little stronger.

"Is it safe to smile now?" I asked through still lips.

"Not a big one, but yes," Royal smiled as he stepped away.

"Thank..."

"Nope," Royal interrupted, still smiling. "Don't say it. It ain't necessary."

"But I want to thank.."

"Nope!" he laughed. I pulled a face. "You'll rip open that lip again, missy!" he admonished.

"Okay, you win, I won't say thank you."

"See that you don't." He winked. "I will head out and get started on your Moon Circle. I suggest you take a nap."

"A nap? But I just got up!"

"And you just split your lip open. Nap!"

"Yes, sir."

Royal kissed me on the top of my hood-covered head and left, his silvery wings dragging lightly on the floor behind him.

6

———

Napping has never been my strong suit. I know it's an important skill that can add years to your life, blah, blah, blah, but I've never really been into it. It didn't feel necessary in my human life, and now that I was an immortal Traveller, it seemed even less useful. But Royal knew what he was talking about. So I gave his order a try and went to see if I could get some day-sleep.

I wasn't sure if it was Traveller magic or brilliant architectural design, but every room in Royal's home was always cool and pleasant. A gentle breeze flowed through the windows, making every room that awesome combo of perfect temperature and fresh air. My room was no exception. I stacked my pillows, so I was sitting up a little; it helped take the pressure off my wings and stretched out on the bed. The cotton wrappings I wore were all the blanket I needed, and within minutes of lying down, I was fighting to keep my eyes open. Begrudgingly admitting to myself that Royal was right about me needing a nap, I pulled a bit of my headscarf over my eyes and drifted off to sleep.

I dreamed. Not wing visions, actual dreams. And not

dreams, more like nightmares. I'd been dealing with them off and on since I'd woken up in Royal's home. Snippets of the City of Caves, the battle with Mhyr, hearing Archer's muffled screams. A rich pageantry of painful crap too fresh in my heart to ignore. I could feel the pounding of a hundred minions throwing themselves against the wall of Mhyr's dome, and I could feel her shaking me; it felt so real, so very real.

I woke with a start; hands were on my shoulders, I cried out and smacked with my useless stick arms at whoever held me.

"Phoenix, Phoenix," a voice whispered, "it's me, Royal." A hand gently pulled my headscarf from my eyes, Royal's hand. "Please calm down, you'll hurt yourself."

I looked up at him and tried to catch my breath. I could feel sweat on my forehead. It burned. I dragged a glove-covered hand across it.

"Hey," I said with a strained voice. "I'm sweating; I haven't done that in a while."

I looked down at my glove. It was tinged scarlet. So I was sweating, but it was bloody, great.

"That's good." Royal didn't notice the glove. He sat down at the end of the bed and smiled, but it didn't go all the way to his eyes.

"What's wrong?" I propped myself up higher on my pillows, grabbed a cloth from the nightstand and dabbed at the drops of blood-sweat on my brow.

I watched Royal, honestly expecting him to say 'nothing's wrong,' and just talk about the moon ceremony some more, but he sat silently and looked at the floor for a very long time.

"You're freaking me out, Royal. What's up?"

"You have visitors."

"What?" My jaw dropped, and then my gut turned in what I hoped was excitement. "Archer? He found me?" I tried to smile, and the cut on my lip smarted. I quickly put my cloth against it. "He can't see me like this. Not yet. After the moon stuff. I need more time."

I moved to rise from the bed and Royal placed a large hand on my leg, stopping me.

"Not Archer."

"Then who?" My gut dropped, disappointment bringing tears to my eyes. I may not want Archer to see me like this, but I desperately wanted to see Archer.

"Well, two minions."

"Seriously?" I asked. Archer momentarily forgotten. "How did they find me?"

"Well, one of them said he'd been tracking you for so long it was second nature to him."

"Sid." Another flip, my gut was getting quite the workout this morning.

"Yeah, that's his name," Royal looked surprised. "You know him then?"

"Yep."

Royal knew the complete story of what happened in the City of Caves, and that technically, I was now the leader of the minions. He'd taken the entire story in and then said, 'well, you got to heal first,' and never mentioned it again.

"Sid found me when I was living as a human and helped me find my wings."

"Oh, he's that one," Royal's face turned grim. "And then he betrayed you to the Guard."

"And then I saved him in the Caves."

"You don't do things by halves, do you?" Royal whistled. "Well, he's tracked you down again, and they want to talk to you. I said I'd have to talk to you first before I brought them anywhere near."

"Who's the other one?"

"Spin."

"Oh," a tiny gasp escaped my lips "I haven't seen him since..." A tear rolled down my cheek; I wiped it away with my increasingly crimson coloured towel. "How does he look?"

"He's got a big scar across his belly, but otherwise he's fine. He grabbed Sid and held him back at one point, strong little fella."

"Why did he have to do that?"

"Well, Sid was pretty amped up, and when I said he couldn't come straight to you, he tried to fight me."

If I'd had eyebrows, they would have risen.

"Sid can fight, I'm surprised Spin could hold him."

"I'm not saying it was easy for the little guy, but he did it."

"Do you know what they want?"

"To take you back to Guard."

"What!?" This time I did spring from the bed.

"No, not like that. To claim your seat. You're their leader, remember?"

"Oh, shit."

"My thoughts exactly."

7

———

Royal went out to collect the two minions and bring them back to his home. I couldn't be out in the direct sun, so it was the only choice. I asked Royal if he was worried about giving them permission to enter his home and he grumbled something about being able to handle anybody, so I let it go.

After Royal left, I spent some time in front of the mirror adjusting my clothes. Clothes being the technical term for the strips of cloth I had lashed around myself. I debated what to do with my skull and face region. Do I cover it up and let them wonder, although my eyes still looked hideous, or do I go out to meet them with my head held high and let them deal with my meaty rawness? I went with both, drape my head and lower face, then pull back the cloth after a few minutes of conversation. I wanted an honest reaction to my appearance. So far only Royal had seen me. He kept telling me I didn't look that bad, but I suspected he wasn't being completely honest.

I was still fussing with my headscarf when I heard Royal usher in Sid and Spin.

"Where is she? We must see her immediately."

"Calm yourself, Sid."

Their voices cut through my heart. I hadn't heard either of them in what felt like forever. In human terms, it had only been a few days since I'd left Spin in that tunnel, and only a few months since I'd seen Sid in the Circle of the Guard, where he betrayed me. Why are all my relationships so complicated? You'd think being a half-human, half-immortal time travelling raw meat covered humanoid with wings would be easy. Ah, sarcasm.

"She'll be out in a moment; I'm sure she heard you squawking."

"I do not squawk."

"Yes," I said, "you do."

I had whispered from the shadows of the hallway, and all three men froze. I moved forward slowly, staying in the shadows.

"Sid and Spin. I like those names together; you sound like a children's show."

"My lady," Spin spoke in a hushed whisper. "It is so good to see you again." He bowed low.

"It's good to see you too, both of you." I had reached the edge of the shadow; beyond this point was the bright living room where they'd be able to see all that I now was. I stopped on the edge of the shadow. I couldn't bring myself to step into the light.

"How did you find me?"

"I felt your power last night," Sid said. "I've spent most of my life tracking you, Phoenix. I know your signature."

When he said my name, something in my heart twitched, and a tear escaped my eye. It stung my cheek, and I exhaled sharply, my gloved hand snapping up to wipe it away.

"My lady, are you hurt?" Spin took a step forward, but Royal placed a hand on his shoulder.

"She'll come out when she's ready, boys."

"Yes, I am hurt." My stomach clenched. "I am very hurt. But I will heal."

I tried to take a deep breath, but at that moment my ribs weren't capable of movement. "To hell with this," I muttered to myself and stepped forward, pulling back my hood as I moved out into the light.

Their reactions were interesting. Royal had placed a preemptive hand on both their shoulders, but neither of them moved. They looked me up and down, their eyes flickering quickly, taking in my raw face and scanning over my mummy-wrapped body. Sid's face scrunched into a tight look of anger while Spin's eyes stretched open like giant saucers.

"If your eyes get any wider, Spin, they'll fall out," I tried to laugh, but it sounded dry and papery. "Sid, you can relax. I will get better."

They both looked unconvinced; I crouched down in front of them.

"Look closely, and you'll see the skin starting to heal," I blinked at them. "And I have eyelids now, which is huge." I smiled a little overzealously and opened the cut at the corner of my mouth again. "Dammit." Royal tossed me a clean cloth, and I dabbed at the wound. "Sorry, this one keeps opening up. Gotta rein in the smiling. Or do it with half my mouth." I raised one side of my face in a mock smile. Spin giggled.

"Stop it!" Sid's voice was harsh. "Stop trying to minimize this situation."

"Excuse me?" Thank god my eyelids had grown back, or my eyeballs would have been on the floor with Spin's.

"I know you, Phoenix. I know you better than I know any other creature in the Void. I have been searching for you since the dreadful blast at the City of Caves, and when I felt your power last night, I knew something was wrong. You felt different, not whole. And here you are, burned beyond recognition, raw flesh stretched over bone. It is shocking, disturbing, and you crack jokes? What is wrong with you?"

Sid's words were cut off by a large glob of phlegm that had dislodged while he ranted. He coughed and hacked. Royal went to the kitchen and got him a glass of water. I stepped back and waited until Sid's coughing had subsided before I spoke.

"Watch it, Sid." He looked at me sharply, but his mouth was full of water so he couldn't respond. "You do not get to judge how I respond to something that is happening to me. This is my healing process; this is what my people do. We burn, and we are healed. It is our cycle, and I will do and say whatever I need to to get through this process. If you find my appearance disturbing, that's your problem, not mine. I didn't ask you here, and I'm not keeping you here." My power was rising; a dark flame flickered around my heart. "You can't handle my behaviour? You betrayed me to the Guard and disappeared after that battle, and still, I saved you from Greldrom! You speak of the Caves; you have no idea what I went through there. After I had chopped off the head of Greldrom, I had them take you first from the wall!" I stalked across the room and threw open the front door. "If you can't handle me, then leave! Go now and never cross my path again!"

My voice echoed around the room. The silence afterwards was deafening. Spin cried, softly, as softly as a phlegm-filled minion can. Sid just stared at me, his breathing the smoothest I'd ever heard from him. After a long moment of him staring and me holding onto the door with as tight a grip as my bony hand could handle, Sid wordlessly handed his glass to Royal and walked towards me. He stood before me and took my free hand in his. The smooth glove looked strange against his flakey skin. He cradled my hand, lovingly, and I was transported back to my apartment all those years ago when he would curl up with on the couch and watch movies, or sit in my room all night just to make sure I was okay. There were tears in his eyes when he looked at me. It broke my heart, but I didn't say a word.

"I am so sorry," his voice was soft, barely above a whisper. "I was just so worried about you and rather than tell you that, I chose anger. You are resilient beyond my imagination, you always have been." He kissed my gloved hand. "I have made so many mistakes in my quest to keep you safe. It's taken me this long to realize that you didn't need that from me. You have a warrior's heart. You always have." He let go of my hand and stood formally before me. "I am your servant, and maybe one day, I will be your friend again. Please accept my apology."

"Ah, Sid," I felt so weary, like my bones had leaked out all their important juices. "Why does it have to be so hard?" I closed the door. "I accept your apology. I have a lot of questions for you that I'll need suitable answers for, but they can wait. Let's sit down and talk through all this Guard business first."

"Very good, my lady."

I turned to see Royal and Spin watching the show. Royal with his usual smirk, Spin drenched with tears.

8

———

"You look great, Spin," I put a hand on his shoulder, and he beamed. "I was worried about you."

"Thank you, Phoenix," he patted his scar. "You did the hard work."

"Let's just keep that part to ourselves for a little while."

"Right."

We both looked at Sid.

"Right," he nodded.

I'd have to trust Sid to keep his mouth shut. Spin had taken a blade to the gut when he helped me find Greldrom, aka Big G, in the City of Caves. I'd been able to heal him before I'd chopped off Big G's head. Healing across the species was a big no-no in the Void and part of the reason the Guard had Banished me. But I was bigger and stronger now, well not right now, while I'm a beef-jerky covered frame of sticks, but when healed I'd be way too powerful for the Guard to push around. I hoped.

"So what happened after I exploded?" I made it deliberately light-hearted. Was I testing Sid even after I accepted his apology? Who me?

"The enormous dome the silver lady trapped you in broke apart and melted into the ground," Spin's eyes filled with memory. "All the minions tried to rush in, but the blast was too powerful and threw us back. There was smoke and flame everywhere. We couldn't breathe. So Rogmesh told us all to go back to the Caves for safety. So we did." He looked at me earnestly. "We wanted to get to you, but it was too dangerous!"

"I understand, Spin. You did the right thing. What happened to the big silver lady?"

"The Archer dragged her away," Sid spoke. His eyes were hard. "She was badly hurt."

"Good," I grunted. Royal nodded.

"Rumour has it that The Archer brought her before his people and Challenged her."

"What does that mean?" I asked. I knew enough about Travellers to know the capital C in Challenge was a given.

"I do not know. Their people are very secretive." Sid paused, "And violent. Whatever it is, it cannot be good."

"So was I just on the ground during all of this?"

"It all happened very fast," Spin replied. "We moved back into the caves so quickly."

"I think I can answer that," Royal spoke. He shifted in his chair, and his wings unfurled a little. "When I got there, you were lying at the bottom of a big crater, no more than a smoking skeleton. No one was around, and it looked like the force of your blast had caused a rock slide in the area. There were piles of rubble everywhere."

"Yes," Sid interjected, "after some time, we sent a few minions to check the scene, but rubble blocked the entrance to our caves. It took us a few hours to dig out and by that time you were gone."

"Well, I scooped her up right away and brought her back here."

"Okay, so if I may recap for my slightly crispy brain; I exploded, it forced the minions to take cover in the caves, Archer dragged Mhyr off to some silver person tribunal, and Royal found me and brought me here."

"That's about it," Royal confirmed.

"So what happens now?" I looked at Sid and Spin. "Why are you here?"

I knew why. Royal had told me. I was the new leader of the minions. I'd felt the title upon me the moment I'd separated Big G's head from his body.

"You are our leader," said Spin.

"Yeah, but I'm hardly in a state to lead," I replied.

"Without a leader, the minions will descend into anarchy and chaos; chaos that could threaten the Void itself," Sid explained.

"Oh, that's just great." Sarcasm, my trusty friend.

"The Guard sent an envoy," Sid continued, "They requested that our leader presents themselves to the Guard and take their seat."

"Who was in the envoy?"

"Mastyx and his cronies."

"Ah yes, Tweedle Pervert and Tweedle Violent."

"Um, I don't think those are their names," Spin looked confused.

"It's a human joke," I replied.

"Oh."

"You must make an appearance," Sid interrupted. "In your current state it will be difficult, but the Guard will get increasingly aggravated the longer you delay. And the more aggravated they become, the more unpredictable."

"By which you mean Cosima."

Royal shot up from his chair with such force his wing slapped the side of my head.

"Ow!" I rubbed my skull gently, the flesh wiggling under my hand.

"Sorry about that," Royal muttered. He stood completely still for a moment before rousing himself. "I just realised you hadn't had lunch. I'll get on with it." He walked swiftly to the kitchen. I looked over at Spin who shrugged as if to say 'he's your friend.'

"Yes, Cosima," Sid said.

Sid was harder than I remembered. His time held by the Guard and then by Big G must have been very difficult for him. I wanted to feel compassion for him, but it was hard. He had betrayed me to the Guard, whether by choice or because Yeren had dragged him into her web of crappiness, it still had almost gotten me killed.

"Ignore her too long, and Cosima will come for you," Sid continued. "And she will use your refusal to appear as an excuse to Challenge you. Something that in your current state you have no hope of surviving."

"Right."

"Lunch."

"That was fast," I smiled; Royal's eyes were tense, his lips drawn into a straight line. "Thank you."

"It's not much, but it'll do."

Royal placed a plate in my hands. Two rough cut slices of bread spread with mashed avocado and a few strips of bacon he had cooked up the night before. Royal's 'not much' was every brunch place's speciality.

"It looks great." Royal nodded and turned to the minions.

"You two hungry?"

Spin opened his mouth to reply; Sid beat him to it.

"No, thank you."

"Okay," Royal turned towards the door, talking as he went. "I've got stuff to finish up for tonight. I'll be back." And then he was gone.

"Did he seem okay to you guys?" I asked.

"He looked upset about something," Spin replied.

"It does not matter," Sid spoke across Spin. "You have a return to plan; you cannot concern yourself with trivial things."

"Sid, am I going to have to tell you again to watch it? Royal has taken excellent care of me; his emotional state is not 'trivial.'"

"I am sorry, I misspoke."

"You've been doing a lot of that lately." His eyes flashed, but he didn't answer back. "We are a long way from those first days I Travelled with you. And I have survived a great deal more without you by my side. I don't want to pull the leader card, but you need to treat me with more respect."

"Yes, my lady."

This friendship was quickly going from rekindled to kindling. I so did not have the energy for this. I took a deep breath. I could feel every one of my ribs straining against it. Could I join the Guard? Was I strong enough? Physically the answer was a screaming no, but my power, could my power stand up against the others? Cosima was a petulant siren I'd already had the pleasure of besting, and Mastyx was a snake man who seemed to be secretly on my side, so no need to worry about those two. Silverwood was incredibly powerful, scary powerful, but he had helped me find the Archer. Well, sort of; we'd both thought that portal would go to him, but it turned out to be a one-way ticket to the silver people's torturous stronghold. Bad times, real bad times. The only way I'd gotten out of that one alive was because Mhyr had helped me. And then she tried to kill me. Then there was the leader of the yetis, Wendiga. I had had little interaction with him, but he looked like some sort of cryptid biker, so I will hedge my bets and say I can't take him.

The last member of the Guard is The Archer. Archer. My Archer. We hadn't seen each other since that night in the City of Caves, and as far as I knew we were keeping our relationship a secret for the time being. If I showed up at the Circle of the Guard looking like this and it was the first time he'd seen me, could he handle that? Could we both handle that? My heart ached for him, but I just couldn't bring myself to let him see me like this. I freaked out when I looked in the mirror. How could I ask more from him?

Meeting with the Guard to take my seat would be a sticky maze of do's and don'ts and political posturing. I needed to be stronger. I needed a few more days. I needed to see Archer. How could I be so cold as to make him deal with seeing my grotesque appearance for the first time in public? He must be so worried about me. I owed him a sneak peek before I took this show on the road.

"I will go to the Guard in three days."

I had been quiet for so long that my voice made Spin jump. Sid did not move; he was as still and silent as a rock.

"I will do the full moon healing here, tonight."

"That's a relief," Royal's voice called from the doorway as he strolled back into the room. He looked much better for his brief time outside.

"And then tomorrow I will return to my home."

"What?" Royal rushed forward. "You won't be completely healed!"

"I know, Royal." I took his fleshy palm in my gloved collection of sticks. "And I won't get fully healed here. I need to go home to my healing circle to really get things cooking, but I won't be strong enough for the Travel until after the full moon."

"Right." He pulled his hand away and sat down heavily in the chair beside me, his pleasant mood slipping away.

"And then I will call Archer."

All three of them went silent. What is about men? Doesn't matter the species, they've all got issues with legit alphas. Oh, Sid fancied himself an alpha, but he couldn't keep Yeren in line. Royal spent most of his time alone, which didn't give him much leadership practice, and Spin... Actually, Spin looked completely okay with it. Huh, Spin was proving to be quite the well-adjusted minion.

"May we accompany you?" Spin asked. "It would be best to arrive at the Circle with a few minions by your side."

"That's an excellent idea." It also made me think of something. "Should I go to the Caves first? Do the minions need to see me before I see the Guard?"

"That would be advisable," Sid rolled the words out slowly, but not quite mockingly. I ignored him and added another day to my plan.

"All right, in four days I will go see the Guard. Day one," I stuck out a bony fabric covered finger, "Full moon healing. Day two, healing at my place." Another wrapped finger. "Day three, call Archer, and day four," I stuck out the fourth finger. Spin's eyes widened. I looked down to see the wrappings on my arm had come loose. A few inches of beef-jerky raw meat goodness was sticking out. "And day four," I wrapped it again as I spoke. "We go to the City of Caves."

"An excellent plan," Sid's voice was nearly as dry as my bones.

9

I t was a long day waiting for the moon to rise. Lots of pacing to pass the time as the sun beat down on the landscape, forcing my fragile skin to stay inside. And then there were two minions to entertain. Well, one, Spin. Sid slinked off to somewhere, and we didn't see him for a few hours. Very fishy. Where could he possibly go in the desert?

Royal kept going out to work on the Moon Circle, coming back in every few hours to force me to eat and then to take a nap. I resisted the napping until later in the afternoon. Spin declared himself my guard and took up a post outside my bedroom door.

There was no guile in Spin. You looked into his moist little eyes and what you saw was the truth. He wasn't thinking about other things, or some great plan, he was just present with you. It was very Zen. Or the biggest con job of all time. There was a cynical part of me that was waiting for him to rip off his mask and reveal that he was Big G, brought back to life by some dark minion magic. But it was a tiny part. I was more worried about Sid and what the hell he was doing with himself. Sid was always a little edgy, a little tightly wound, but after the torture by Greldrom, he seemed extra dark.

I closed the door to my room and heard Spin slide down it to settle on the floor outside. I listened there for a few moments and soon his normally ragged breaths had settled into a gentle rhythm. My little guard was asleep. It was just as well; he'd probably been up for over a day Travelling with Sid as they searched for me. Sid. Hmm.

I did something I hadn't done since I'd found myself in this room all those days ago. I locked the bedroom door. And then I walked over to the window and with some effort closed the giant shutters that flanked it. They hadn't been used in years and screeched as I pulled at them. I heard Spin give a harrumph from outside the door, but he didn't wake up. I closed the shutters and slid the three locks that lined the joining into place. Satisfied that I was as secure as I would get, I laid out on my bed and tried to get some sleep.

I hadn't been asleep very long when something woke me. Some kind of sound. At first, I tried to go back to sleep, but the sound kept going. A scratching sound. A light scratching sound at my window. I slid as silently as I could from the bed, which is difficult when you have little in the flesh department. Ample thighs help to soften the creaks of a bed, and right now my ample thighs were nowhere to be found. I missed them.

I walked around the periphery of the room, staying close to the wall. I was hoping I could get a glimpse through the shutters who was out there scratching, scratching at my chamber door. Sorry, chamber window. Sorry, bedroom wall hole.

The slats were too tightly milled for me to see through, so I went with Plan B.

"Who's out there?"

I said it as sharply as I could while standing right next to the window. Whoever was on the other side yelped. Point for Phoenix.

"It's me."

Sid. What was he doing?

"Who's me?" Wake me up, and I will screw with you.

"Sid."

"What do you want, Sid? I was sleeping."

"I wanted to talk to you without the prying eyes of the others."

"You wanted to get me alone?"

"Yes."

"Right. So what do you want to talk about?"

"Are you going to open the window?"

"I may open it; I may not. That depends on what you want to talk about."

"What I want to talk about is not best bellowed through a closed window."

"Oh, Sid, you're hardly bellowing and the longer you stall on the topic sentence of this proposed tete a tete, the more I don't want to open the window. So I'll ask you one last time; what do you want to talk about?"

I could hear him breathing on the other side of the shutters. Underneath his rough breaths was the unmistakable silence of someone thinking really, really hard.

"I believe you are in danger."

"Come on, Sid, I've been in danger for weeks, you'll need to do better than that."

"I believe that you were allowed to kill Greldrom, that someone on the Guard used you to get rid of him."

That got the shutters open.

10

———

"What are you talking about?" I pulled the last lock and sat down on the deep windowsill; Sid took a seat opposite me.

"No one has been inside the City of Caves who is not a minion. No one. It has never happened. In all our endless time, a non-minion has never set foot inside our most powerful stronghold. And yet, in the space of days, you are taken to the City in the Trees, and then allowed to go to the very bowels of the Caves. It just isn't probable. Possible, yes, but most definitely not probable."

"I didn't know that."

"How could you? We minions guard our secrets well."

"So I was set up?"

"It is a possibility. How else could you have gotten into the Caves?"

"Well, Archer and I didn't really ask permission. We took out the two minions guarding the entrance and then we hacked our way through." I shuddered. It had been horrible down there. So much evil emanating from the walls. It had triggered something in Archer, and he'd gone totally nuts down there. It had gotten so bad that he'd run away from me, leaving me alone in the passages. If Spin hadn't been there to help me... Well, it wouldn't have been much fun.

"Wait," I snapped from the vision. "Do you think Spin was in on it?"

"It is a possibility."

"That's super annoying, Sid. Just say what you mean."

"No," he sighed. "I do not think Spin was in on it. He is too innocent. How he held onto that innocence while in that terrible place is a mystery. I do not think the minions themselves, en masse, knew about the plan, and most would not know that you were the first non-minion to enter the Caves. They are too stupid to remember our lore."

"So it was someone higher up. But who? There's only Big G ruling you guys, yes?"

"Oh," Sid giggled; it was a combination of coughing and gagging. He hacked up a wad of phlegm and spat it into the sand. "I had forgotten your nickname for him. Very funny." He wiped his mouth with the back of his hand. "Yes, there is only Big G. So someone must have coerced him into relaxing the magical barriers around the entrance. But who?"

"Well, they probably told him they wanted me dead and that he'd be rewarded."

"Rewards wouldn't hold much weight with Big G; he has everything he could want. No, I think he would be in it solely for your death."

"Damn."

"Yes, damn," Sid nodded.

"So who would conspire with him?" I stood up a little too quickly and felt something on my left side tear. "Shit!"

Blood blossomed across my torso. Without thinking of who was in the room, I ripped the cloth from my chest and grabbed a clean towel from the pile by my bed. The tear was a small one but bled freely. I pressed the towel to the wound and sat down gingerly on the edge of the bed. I looked up at Sid; he hadn't moved, but tears streamed down his face, splashing onto the stucco. I realised then that my entire torso was fully exposed. The visible ribs, the shadow of my lungs, the deep concave curve where my stomach had once been. I didn't say anything, and neither did Sid. After a moment of silence, we continued with our conversation.

"Did they expect me to survive?"

"No, my lady, I do not think they did." Then he slid off the windowsill and disappeared into the sand.

I couldn't believe I'd let him see so much of my body. I had planned to keep that from as many people as possible. I still wasn't sure I could let Archer see me so raw and bloody. But Sid had taken it in with a good deal of grace. The tears were genuine. I could see that. So maybe his offer of friendship was too. I felt like I could trust him, but I'd felt that way before and gotten burned. Argh. There were too many things to figure out, and I needed to focus on the night ahead. If I had any hope of putting some more meat on my bones, I had to get my head on straight.

11

———

I took a quick nap. It seemed important considering I'd be up all night howling at the moon. Well, not howling, just letting the moon's glorious light ignite the healing properties within me. Well, that's how Royal described it. He could be quite the poet when he wanted to be. I was contemplating a bath to wash the dried blood from my torso when there was a knock at the door.

"Miss Phoenix, you have a visitor!" Spin called through the thick wood.

"Who is it, young Spin?" I could almost hear the smile spread across his face as I played along.

"It is the one they call Royal."

I unlocked the door and found Royal standing exactly two paces behind Spin who stood before the door, his chest high and his chin forward.

"Your visitor, my lady." He bowed and stepped aside.

"Thank you, Spin. Could you find Sid and see what he's up to? It'll be dark soon."

"Yes, Miss Phoenix." He smiled, and dropping to his hands and feet, scampered up the hall.

"They sure can move when they want to," Royal said as he watched Spin's awkward gait.

"You should see them in a forest. It's like they melt around things."

"I don't doubt it," Royal looked at me. "Why is there blood on your clothes?"

"I moved too quickly, and something tore. It bled more than the wound warranted, though; it was only a tiny cut."

"That's a good sign!" Royal took a seat on the window ledge where Sid had been speculating only a few hours before. "It means the blood flow is coming back."

"Well, that's just great," I sat down slowly on the bed, but the cut still stung. "The whole raw nerve thing is getting old though."

"Hopefully tonight will seal some frayed edges."

"That would be great. I'm tired of feeling every single bone in my feet with every step I take."

"You will need better shoes when you leave here."

"I've got lots of great shoes at home; I just need to wrap my feet up well for the journey."

Royal grunted a noncommittal response and looked at his hands for a few moments.

"So you are going home." It wasn't a question, and it held a level of resignation that made me sad.

"I have to, Royal."

"Why?"

"There is a space in my home that I designed specifically for healing myself. I guess I used to get hurt a lot before my time as a human. It's a circle deep inside a greenhouse I built in my house. I know if I get there I can speed this healing process along. I'm not strong enough to Travel yet, so I need to do the moon healing tonight, but after that, I've got to get home. The circle there knows my body; it will know what to do to get me better." I looked at the dried blood on the strips of cloth that wrapped around me. "I think I'll need a few treatments though."

"Makes sense." He paused. "Will you visit me?"

Oh! So that's what this was about. Royal thought he'd never see me again. For all of his crotchety old man mutterings, he liked the company. Liked my company. And I liked him.

"Of course I will," I slid my boney ass onto the window ledge beside him. "Royal, you are the only person I've met who is just like me. We are two of the same species in a world where most of these guys operate in the thousands, or at least the hundreds. We need each other. We need to stay close." I thought back to what Sid had said. Someone out there still wanted me dead. "I don't think the danger is anywhere close to being over for me. Not just because I look like a skinned rabbit. There's something dark out there that's still got its eyes on me." I shuddered, and Royal put his arm around me. I curled into his shoulder as his wings wrapped around us both.

"I'm there for you, Phoenix. You just say the word."

"Word." He laughed; I could feel it right through my battered body. It loosened something in my chest. "Wait a second," I sat up. Whatever had come loose was now banging away in my chest. "Something's moving." I took his hand and put it on my chest. If I still had breasts, it would have been way inappropriate, but I was just a ribby meat wall. "What is that?"

Royal sighed, and a single silver tear moved quickly down his cheek.

"That's your heart, honey. It's beating again."

12

———

Finding out that you've been living without a beating heart would mess with most people's brains. Fortunately, I am not most people. Unfortunately, I am far too used to the crazy crap going on in my life, so the news that my heart had returned to its steady rhythm was only a mild shock. A shock that made my heart stop, but after a few thumps from Royal, got moving again.

Once Royal was sure my heart would not stop again, he ordered me to take a bath and get dressed. The sun was disappearing below the horizon, and I needed to be out in the Moon Circle soon. I bathed as quickly as I could, which was kind of gross. Running my stick fingers over my meat covered legs and barely there torso was not fun. But I rinsed off the dried blood and carefully patted myself dry. I did not need another tear this close to the moon.

I picked up the robe Royal had left for me. A poncho. His word, a poncho. What Royal calls a poncho, I call a tent. It was big and grey with no slits for my arms or my wings, and a big hood that covered my head and most of my face. It was so long it pooled on the floor, which made walking slightly more challenging than my stick feet could handle.

Now dried and draped, I made my tent-like way out to the living room. All three men were sitting around the fire with strained looks on their faces.

"Cheer up, it might not happen," I said from deep within my grey hood. Spin glanced up at me and yelped.

"Oh! I am sorry, miss; it's just, you look like..."

"I look like a tent of nightmares," I waved my arms under the robe. "Enter if you dare! Ooooo! Ooooo!"

"All right, that's enough," Royal said it playfully, but there was an undercurrent of tension to his words.

"You're right. I could play tent of nightmares all night, and then where would we be?"

"Hilarious, Phoenix." He moved to the door. "Let's get you outside."

"Okay." I waved to Sid and Spin, who sat on the couch in various displays of tension. "I'll see you guys later."

Once outside, Royal seemed to go back to his usual relaxed self.

"The circle is just over that rise there." He pointed to a dark mass in the near distance. "Just walk in a straight line, and you can't miss it."

"You're not coming with me?" panic just edging into my voice.

"No, darling. You can do it all by yourself." He smiled and then reached up and pulled the hood back from my flesh-less head. "Nobody out here to see you, let it all hang out."

"Okay." If I'd had real lips, I'd have stretched them into a very thin line. "I don't like this."

"You're not supposed to," Royal placed a hand gently on my shoulder. "If you were supposed to, we'd be burning up all over the place."

"All of us, being the two of us," I said.

"Yeah, just the two of us. Now get going before you miss the moon."

"Where is the moon?" The sky was dark save for a few twinkling stars. "And how am I going to see where I'm going?"

"The moon will show up."

"Seriously?"

"Yep, it'll show up."

"All right then." I took a few steps towards the rise. "Thank you, Royal, for everything."

"You're welcome." He smiled and then walked back into the house, leaving me alone in the dark with sand between my toe bones.

13

———————

The sand between my toes really freaked me out as I walked. It was literally between my toes. I could feel it swirling around the exposed bones of my feet, sometimes pushing up through the spaces and spilling out over the surface. In sand, feet are meant to act as paddles. Mine were working like sieves. Getting over the rise was slow work.

It was nice not to wear a big hood over my head. The fresh night air felt wonderful as it slid over the bones of my skull. Twice a big gust came up, and I wished loudly for eyelashes. But the plus of being sinewy was the sand came in and then just fell out.

My head was down when I suddenly noticed that the sand between my foot bones glowed. I looked for the source of the light and found myself face to face with the biggest moon I'd ever seen. Maybe it was a trick of the desert, or maybe it was Traveller magic, but that moon hung so full and so close that I felt I could reach out and run my hand over its rocky surface.

"Whoa."

I am so eloquent.

Tearing my eyes from the moon, I looked around at the circle Royal had fashioned. 'Circle' was an inferior name for the magical space that lay before me. When he said Circle, I pictured a line drawn around an area in the sand and maybe a blanket in the middle for me to rest my bones on. This was so much more than that.

The area was ringed in torches; they hadn't been lit, but the moon provided more than enough light. Royal had placed a torch at each point of a compass, or the hours on the clock. Once I laid in the centre, we would form a kind of moon dial. In the circle's heart was an enormous pool. It was as smooth as glass and shone like an opal in the moonlight. The scene was beautiful and powerful. I could feel it pulling at me.

I slipped out of my robe and let it fall to the sand. The breeze caressed my skin. I took a deep breath and centred myself. I had to be present for this. If I wanted to be strong enough to get home, I needed this to work. I called to the power deep in my belly and felt it there like a pilot light waiting for kindling. Then I stepped forward into the circle of torches.

The moment I crossed into the Circle, all sound ceased. I hadn't noticed the sounds of the desert as I walked, but now that they were gone, the lack of sound pressed in on my ears. I let my robe slip from my shoulders and stepped off the sand, into the moon water. It was cool but not cold, the sand beneath it warm. A pleasant feeling. The power in the water pulled at my memories. My wing stubs twitched, and images of the Void ran behind my eyes. Memories I hadn't yet remembered and maybe never would. Strange. An entire life lived and no memory of it. Maybe that's how a past life feels? I guess technically it was a past life. A life that part of my body had lived without me.

My wing stubs were positively thrumming, and the desert breeze was getting colder by the moment. The moon was growing in size before my very eyes. Soon it would be at its apex. I needed to hurry. I walked out to the centre of the pool and looked up at the moon. It looked to be inches from my face, and I reached out to touch it. As my fingers extended towards the orb, they brushed against something cold and grainy. I pulled my hand back. Had I just touched the moon? No, that was impossible and yet, I had touched something.

I reached out again, slowly this time, and pressed my palm towards the pale grey of the moon's surface and touched rock. I pressed my incomplete hand against the stone, and the moon itself pulsed ever so slightly. This time I did not pull away. I brought my other hand up and stood naked, a collection of sticks and sinew, with both hands pressed against the surface of the moon.

The moon throbbed, and as she did, cold moonlight dripped down my arms, coating every little sliver of flesh clinging to my bones. The bones themselves vibrated. A small contained vibration that held me tight to the moon and asked my bones to grow. Don't ask me how she communicated that, but she did. The moon asked my bones to grow. I took the message to my heart and repeated it like a mantra. My wing stubs heard the call and flapped slowly against my shoulders. The tiny stubs of bone no longer than a pencil stretched as best they could towards the sky, the moon, the great giving orb.

The grey energy of the moon coated my arms and now moved across my shoulders and chest. It ripped right through the flimsy skin covering my ribcage, tearing through the slivers of intercostal muscle. Fresh blood welled up as a scream ripped from my mouth. I tried to pull my hands from the moon, but she held onto me. The pain was incredible, and my knees buckled, the moon's grip on my hands the only thing keeping me upright. I hung there as she invaded my body with her power. Her brilliant grey light plunged into the cavity of my chest and surrounded my heart and lungs. My heart, which had only just started beating again, beat faster and faster under her tutelage. She held my lungs in her power and pushed them to the very edge of their capabilities. Filling and draining them over and over again with oxygen.

I could do nothing. I was along for the ride, and that knowledge filled me with calm. As peace washed through my mind, my body relaxed, and the pain felt less intense. Now finished with my heart and lungs, the moon worked her magic through my torso, moving down through my internal organs. I struggled to my feet. I hurt. I felt like my body was running a marathon as I stood under the light of the moon. But I could handle it; I could ride the waves of pain. Whatever was happening here was healing me. I would not resist it.

The light had now coated my pelvis and was crawling down my thighs, encouraging the tissue, vibrating the bone. It passed over my knees, and I let out a slight cry as it swirled around the crispy cartilage and through the joint itself. It moved down my shins where I was only bone, and doubled the vibration, I looked down hoping to see the flesh regrow, but all I could see was the bright light of the moon coating me. I watched as that light travelled down my shins and touched the surface of the water.

Instantly the entire pool became a great glowing mass of grey light. The torches around the circle began one at a time to flare into life, their flames bright grey. The entire area was awash in the moon's power. It forcibly reminded me of the Void, my land, the place that birthed me. I missed it. I missed the grey undulating ground and the cool dark streams. I missed the trees that swayed without winds. I missed the sky, the vast grey sky that I had spent a lifetime flying through with my brightly coloured wings. I missed it all.

A single tear fell from my eye and dropped unheeded to the pool below. As it struck the surface a swirl of pink, my power, flowed out through the sea of grey. Swirling and multiplying, it filled the pool. The light in the torches faded from grey to pink, and as they did so, the moon loosened her grip on my hands. I did not hold on; I lifted my hands from its great surface and stretched my arms wide. The moon's power caressed me, and soon I found myself falling backwards, most gently, to rest in the pink and grey swirling pool. The last thing I saw as I drifted off to sleep was the moon shrinking in size as she made her way over the horizon.

14

I woke to the fresh pale light of morning. I could see my breath in the air, a misty cloud against the crispness of the sky. I was warm and relaxed but didn't know why. A bird sounded in the distance, and I suddenly remembered where I was. The desert. I sat up slowly and as the water streamed from my body, the morning air rushed in to surround my flesh.

Flesh.

I had flesh.

I held up my hands. They had meat on them. My fingers could move! I looked down at my legs and feet; they were now corded with muscles. No skin or fascia, just solid red muscles running down my legs and wrapping around my toes. I resembled a giant piece of red liquorice, but it was a step from beef jerky. I ran my fingers over my stomach; there was flesh now there too. I ran my hands up over my chest, my breasts hadn't returned, but I had pecs.

I rose from the water and looked around. The torches were black and cold, having burned themselves down to just stubs above the sand. Stubs! I had almost forgotten my wing stubs. I looked over my shoulder and saw that where I had once had tiny sticks, I now had large webs of bone. There were bits of tendon and even smaller bits of flesh holding them together. It was fantastic.

I walked to the edge of the pool, revelling in the fullness of my feet and the ease with which I powered through the sand. Man, it felt good. The breeze was gentle on my new flesh, and the sun was drying me. I picked up my robe from the side of the pool. I was still a little damp and decided to walk naked part of the way back.

I walked over the sandy rise, but misjudged my newly formed feet and tumbled down into the sand. This was when I realised naked was an awful idea. Falling didn't really hurt, but when I got up and looked down at myself, a fine layer of sand covered me from calf to sternum. I sighed and made my way back up the hill to the moon pool.

The sun was getting hot, and I did not need a sunburn. So I washed off the sand as quickly as I could and then rushed myself into the robe. As I drew the hood up over my head, it flopped quicker than I expected and I had to shut my eyes against the onslaught of cloth. It was at this point I noticed I now had functioning eyelids. Which made me smile. Which then made me realize I had lips! I ran my fleshy fingers, which still had no fingerprints; you need skin for fingerprints, over my new lips. They were skinny and flat, but they covered my teeth and let me smile. I had to get to a mirror to see how all this was looking. Wrapped up tight against the sun, I made my way quickly and carefully back to Royal's house.

Spin was sleeping on a pile of sand by the door. He had burrowed down into it, so only his head and hands were visible. The sand rose and fell with his breath, little trails of sand shifting as he moved. It was kind of cute, his little bald flaky head poking up from the sand, a little trail of drool and snot streaming from his face.

"Good morning, Spin," I whispered to him.

"Hmm-mmm," he mumbled and then snuggled deeper into the sand. I couldn't leave him out here. In a few hours he'd bake like a ham. I tapped him gently on the head.

"Spin, it's time to get up."

"Hmm-mmm." More mumbling. More action needed.

"Spin! Get up!" He moved so quickly that sand exploded from his body, I held my hood closed against the onslaught. I did not need more sand stuck to me.

"Ah! Ah! Ah!" Spin randomly yelled as he jumped up, then he saw me. "Oh, Phoenix, oh, I'm so sorry, I didn't hear you come home."

As he babbled, the front door of Royal's place came crashing open. I didn't have to turn around to know who was rushing up behind me, Sid had a very distinct gate, that hand and foot shuffle thing I knew so well.

"You are back!" he cried as he came to a complete and surprisingly gentle stop at my feet.

"I'm back," I said from deep within my hood. The sun was getting higher and hotter, and I was not burning this fresh face flesh. Say that three times fast.

"It did not go well?" Sid asked.

"Why do you say that?" I asked, slightly incredulous.

"You have your face hidden."

"Even if it had worked well," I shook my head, "which it did, I still wouldn't be parading my fresh face around in this bright sun. Do you guys even have sunscreen?" The two minions looked at me like I'd grown another raw meat head.

"Sun screen?" Spin rolled the words around in his mouth.

"Never mind," I muttered.

"Breakfast!" Royal called from the open doorway. How did he know I'd be home?

"Excellent!" Spin cried as he bolted through the door, sand trailing in his wake.

15

———

Royal spooned bacon and eggs onto plates. My stomach was cold and empty, it growled as the smell hit my nostrils.

"That smells amazing," I said, taking a seat at the counter. My hood was still up, and I didn't plan on taking it off soon. I used my fork to fly bits of egg and toast into its cavernous depths. Royal interrupted my egg shovelling.

"Take the hood off."

"Is that an order?"

"I need to see how healed you are."

"Fine." I felt like a pouty teenager. When I finished these eggs, I was so out of here. "You couldn't just let me eat for a few minutes."

"Hood."

I sighed and pulled the hood back. All three men gasped.

"What?" I looked around at their stricken faces. "I couldn't possibly have gotten worse out there."

"No, Phoenix," Sid replied, "not worse technically, just more shocking perhaps."

"Seriously?" I jumped up. "I need to see this." I walked down the hall towards my room, three gentlemen hot on my heels. "Guys, I'm okay, you don't need to babysit me."

"We'll see," Royal muttered.

I entered the room and went straight to the large glass I knew so well.

I didn't look good.

Yes, I had a fresh layer of muscle all over my once bony frame, and yes, I now had eyelid and fingertips and all that good stuff. But what I didn't have was skin. And skin, I learned as I looked at the horror show starring back at me, was the important part. I looked disgusting. I looked inside out. I looked down at the big tent I was wearing and pulled it up, exposing my feet. I gagged and dropped the robe to the floor.

"You don't have to look, my lady," Spin said, crawling forward ever so slowly like he wanted to be close to me, but part of him wanted out of the room. "You can wait until you've healed some more. Maybe at the next moon?"

"No, I need to see this. I need to know what I'm dealing with."

"Are you sure?" Royal's voice was a dry whisper from the doorway.

"This is my body!" I yelled. Fear and pain were getting to me. A deep scream was trying to get out, and I didn't want to let it go. "It's my body," I said more calmly. "If I can't handle it, then I'm fucked."

Spin gasped at the swear, but seriously, this was the time for swearing.

"All right, let me help you." Royal stepped forward and took the robe in his hands. "I'll pull it off as gently as I can, but it might stick to you in a few places."

"Gross." I put my arms up. "Go for it."

Royal did his best, but yes, the fabric stuck to me in a few places as he brought it over my head. There were a few seconds of grey darkness as the voluminous cape-robe-thing flowed over my head and then I was free. I closed my eyes; the breeze hitting my flesh and making me wish I had skin to goose bump.

When I finally opened my eyes, I did throw up. It wasn't much because I had gotten little of the eggs and bacon in me, but throw up I did. My legs buckled and Royal was right there, catching me in the folds of the robe he'd just removed, careful not to touch my raw flesh. Sid and Spin sprang into action and started cleaning up my mess.

I hadn't grasped the severity of my situation until just that moment. When I was a skeleton girl, it had been easy to ignore what was happening, to almost laugh at it. Oh no, you can see my ribs! Or hey, where'd my ass go? Ha ha. It had been too fantastical to believe I was actually alive in that state. It had felt like a dream, walking around bandaged up like some mummy from a black and white movie. But I wasn't in black and white anymore. I was in bright crazy technicolour.

The worst part was my stomach. Every single muscle was visible and as I breathed, a shiny red mass that shifted with every inhalation and exhalation. Every inch of me shone with a gloss of fresh blood. I had a terrible thought and looked down to realize, yep; I was leaving bloody foot-prints. I reached out and touched the wall, leaving a single dot of red behind.

I turned in the mirror and saw that I had an ass again, which was about the only good thing going on at the moment. 'Ass' being the term I would use for the blood-covered chunk of flesh that had formed in my backside region.

My face was bizarre. I could see now why the boys had freaked out when I'd taken off my hood. My eyes were ringed in muscle that moved and twitched when I looked in different directions. My head was covered in strips of muscle that ran away from my eyes and over my skull and then joined the ropier things that covered my back. Bands of muscle stretched from under my eyes towards my mouth, and my lips were surrounded by a ropy loop of meat that pulled and pinched with every word I spoke. As I watched it move in the mirror, I realised I was talking. I shook my head to clear my mind and watched tiny droplets of blood splatter across the floor.

"I will be okay."

"You've said that many times, Phoenix," Sid was quietly wiping up the tiny splatters of blood. "You must focus your mind now. Your kind has survived this many times, so will you." He stopped wiping and looked up at me, a smile on his face. "You are a warrior. This is nothing for you."

There was a look of deep pride on his face, and my wings twitched at my back as I, present me, showed them memories of all that Sid and I had been through; the late nights on my couch watching movies, the stories of his adventures. And then our adventures through the Void: Yeren's cave, the Riders and Baba Yaga, and the stone winged dog things I'd smashed to a million pieces. We'd been through a lot together. And we'd been through a lot while we were apart. I thought back to seeing him hanging from the wall deep in the City of Caves. Bloody, beaten, near death. He had been through some serious stuff while we'd been apart. We both had.

"Did you rat me out to the Guard?" I said the words quietly so only he would hear.

"Phoenix," he hung his head, "I wish I could tell you no,

but yes I did." He looked at me, his eyes cold and dry. "By the time they finished with Yeren she had told them everything. Everything!" The word was a harsh whisper. "I tried to stay strong, to keep my mouth shut. I thought maybe if they just had her words they would think she was lying. But then they brought in Greldrom, and he is," Sid shook his head, "no, was my leader. And he was powerful. He used his horrible techniques on me, he drew the memory from my very soul, and no matter how hard I tried to cast him out, he ran like the wind through my mind and took all he wanted. So yes, I betrayed you to the Guard, and I will take that shame to my grave."

"Whoa." I shook my head again, more blood, more wiping from Sid. "So Big G mind rapes you, and you think that's your fault? You think that means you betrayed me?"

"I did."

"Holy crap, Sid!" I raised my hands in exasperation, and large drops of blood hit Sid's face. "Sorry about that." He wiped them away. "Seriously Sid, I would not hold you responsible for that. He forced you. You didn't have a choice. You tried to keep my Secrets, and he ripped them from your mind. That is not your fault, and that is no reason to stay away from me for all this time." I tried to kneel but my knees squelched, and it grossed me out. "Sid, you were one of my closest friends. I need you in my life. Look at me," I ran my hand over my fleshy mass, and it felt slippery, "I'm a bit of a mess right now. I could use you back in my corner."

"My lady," he stood up to his full height, a big smile spread across his face, "I never left."

"Excellent!" I clapped my hands and felt them squelch together. "So gross." I looked around the room, Royal and Spin had left. "Where is everyone?"

"We're right here." Royal was coming through the door

with Spin behind him. Both were carrying bundles of cloth. "We were getting you some clothes."

"Clothes being the code word for bandages that will cover and absorb my current bloodiness?" I tried to smile, but I think with all the strips of meat crisscrossing over my face the effect was lost.

"Yeah," Royal grimaced, "we've got to do something about that."

16

———

The three of them got to work with me standing in the centre of the room like a strange doll. There was a time when standing nude in front of these guys would have been decidedly odd, but naked goes out the window when you don't have skin. So I stood there and let them look me up and down as they decided on the best way to wrap me up.

"I think we've got to do a layer of the terry cloth for absorption and then cover the entire thing with the thick canvas," Royal said.

"Thing?" I asked. Everyone ignored me.

"Agreed," Sid spoke, "The canvas is thick enough that if she is to bleed through the cotton, it will hide the leaks until she can get better clothing."

"Guys, I just need to get to my place. Once I'm there, I can do another healing, and that should seal up all this juiciness."

"All right then, let's start with the terry cloth," Royal said.

"You mean the towels?" Spin asked.

Good lord, they were going to wrap me in towels.

The procedure took some time. The group decided that the best way to go was to start with my pelvis and torso so they could then sit me down to wrap my legs. The pelvis wrapping part got weird. The three of them looked at each other, unsure of who was to do the actual wrapping. I eventually had to step in and take the cloth, sorry towel, from them and wrap my pelvis myself. I couldn't get the strips of cloth all the way around by myself. And I left bloody handprints on everything I touched, which defeated the purpose entirely. Eventually, Spin shuffled over and did a surprisingly sensitive job of helping me into the bandages. Once he and I had my pelvis wrapped, the others could step in. They made quick work of my torso, legs and arms and then repeated the entire process with the heavy canvas. My wings weren't as bloody as the rest of me, so Royal slipped sheets around each one, tucking the ends into my shoulder wrappings.

We left my head unwrapped. Royal fashioned a large hood out of the canvas and then, using some netting, put a veil over my face.

We stood before the big mirror and surveyed our work.

"You'll do," Royal grunted.

"I look like a mummy from a low budget horror movie," I said.

"Yes," Sid interjected, "it is a highly unusual outfit, but it will serve our purposes."

"I think you look cool!" Spin was the only one smiling. "You look like a space ninja!"

"How do you know what a space ninja looks like?" Sid asked.

"I go to the movies sometimes," Spin quipped.

"Okay guys, the wrapping is complete, and it's time to get a move on." I started down the hall. "Sid, Spin, grab your stuff. Royal, if you could fetch my sword."

"Really?" he asked.

"Well, wrap it up tight and give it to Spin to carry. I don't want any mistaken touches while we're Travelling."

"On it."

I didn't need to pack. I came here with nothing, and I'd leave with just the bandages on my back.

It didn't take the guys long to pack either. They both had their backpacks on and were out the door in minutes. All four of us walked over the rise towards Royal's Travelling point. When we got there, he handed the tightly wrapped sword to Spin who strapped it to his body with a length of rope he pulled from his bag. I turned to Royal.

"Thank you for everything."

"You're welcome."

"I will be back."

"I know." He smiled. "And it'll be sooner than you think." He smiled and walked away.

He left me standing with Sid and Spin. Two trusted companions. Sid the minion that had started it all, and Spin who had helped me when I was knee deep in crap and scrambling around in the City of Caves. Things with Sid seemed to be back on track. Our brief talk in my bedroom, well the two talks we'd had in my bedroom, seemed to have put things back together again.

"My lady?" Sid broke through my thoughts.

"Why so formal?"

"The Names Travel. I feel that from this point on, we should not use your proper name. You are still vulnerable, and if any creature were to track you, I am not confident that Spin and I could protect you."

That was exactly what he'd said to me back in my apartment all those years... Wait, it was only months, or maybe weeks ago? Man, I was getting on Traveller time... Those were the words that started this adventure and here we were embarking on another chapter.

"Good point, Sid. And to be doubly safe, I'll call you Tweedle Dum and Spin, Tweedle Dee."

"I don't believe that will be necessary," Sid grumbled as Spin hid his smile.

"Spin you've got the sword?"

"Yes, ma'am." He clutched it to his chest.

"Well, I'm sure with my wings all jacked up that I'll need to borrow some power from you guys to Travel."

"Then we shall hold hands," Sid instructed. "Then you think of your home, and it will direct our Travel."

Think of my home. That sounded like Silverwood's advice to think of Archer so I could figure out which portal to take. That time I'd ended up balls deep in the silver man stronghold, being 'helped' by the ever terrifying Mhyr. Huh, I wonder if Silverwood had known something like that could happen?

"My lady?" Sid asked, his hand outstretched.

I parked the Silverwood question and took his hand. Spin slid a dry flakey palm into my other hand.

"There's no place like home," I whispered.

Then we Travelled.

17

———

The Travel was a breeze. Maybe because I'm now the leader of the minions', or maybe because Spin and Sid's power is less than my own? I don't know. All I do know is that the three of us landed on our feet in the middle of the forest path, and that ain't half bad.

"Are you guys okay?" I asked as I whipped my head back and forth, checking the area.

"Of course," Sid replied immediately. "We are quite used to Travel."

"That was great!" Spin exclaimed, the muslin-wrapped sword still gripped tightly against his chest. "I've never done that before!"

"You've Travelled, surely, Spin?" I asked.

"Oh yes, but never that far and never with other people!" He was practically bouncing. "I never knew the Time Tunnel could be so colourful!"

"Oh, isn't it always?"

"It is for you, my lady. For others it appears differently," Sid answered.

"Weird..." I looked up the path towards my home. "I guess we'd better get moving."

"Yes," Sid urged.

"Follow me then."

I started off down the path with the two minions behind me. Sid walking on two feet and Spin, who had the sword, was shuffling along with a two-legs-and-an-arm gait. I looked back, and he was definitely dragging behind.

"Sid, can you bring up the rear, please?"

"The rear?"

"Yes, can you walk behind Spin? I don't want him exposed while he's carrying my sword."

"As you wish."

As I waited for them to figure things out, I took in the forest's beauty: the dappled light that broke through the trees, the light bark, the sounds of birds chirping. It was a wonderful spot. I could feel in my bones just what in my past life had brought me to this place. I felt calm here, open and vulnerable, but welcomed at the same time. It was an incredible feeling.

"My lady?" Spin sat at my feet.

"Oh, sorry Spin, I didn't see you there."

He smiled at me. He seemed to be happier and brighter here too.

"Shall we continue?" Sid asked.

"Yes, we're very close."

I led the boys on through the forest, taking care to let its energy in, but not to let it pull me under. I had never felt such a powerful pull from the trees. Maybe I was just more open to it now that I was, well, raw.

We reached the gate, its woven branches covered with a soft layer of moss and lichen. Through the gate, I could see my home: the extensive stone structure and the large greenhouse, the giant wooden door that I could almost fly through, and, settled on the front stoop, my two trusty gargoyles basking in the morning sunlight.

My gargoyles.

Crap, I'd forgotten all about them. They would want to talk to me; they deserved an explanation why I looked so jacked up. But if I brought Spin and Sid in with me, they wouldn't be able to come to life. They'd be stuck as stone and staring at my gross appearance with no explanation. They were loyal friends and helped me out of some serious jams. Heck, it wasn't too long ago they'd dragged me through this very gate as I screamed. They'd taken turns heating themselves up in the fire and snuggling up with me to stop me from getting hypothermia. I owed them an explanation.

"Guys," I turned to the minions, "I need you to wait out here for a little while."

They just stared at me. Spin with a smile and Sid with an unreadable expression.

"There are a few things I need to take care of in there before I can let you in. You know, because once you're in, it's kind of forever."

"We understand," Sid said, although his expression didn't really scream understanding.

"We'll wait right here!" Spin said, and he plopped down on the ground right in front of the gate. Perfectly positioned to watch the gargoyles come to life.

"Maybe you guys should go sit in that shady spot over there?" I pointed to a little grassy area just off the path. "The grass will be way more comfortable."

"Oh, it looks nice," Spin was already moving through the trees.

"Spin," Sid's voice carried in the air, "please give the lady her package."

Spin stopped dead in his tracks and looked down at the bundle he was carrying. He loped back to me and stretched out his arms. I took the tightly wrapped sword from him.

"Thanks, guys. I appreciate it."

"We shall await your return." Sid led Spin out into the forest.

I waited until they were both sitting in the grass, Sid with his back pointed towards me, and then I crossed through the gate.

A little while back I'd run into a bit of trouble with this gate. I had just taken a long soak, long soak being a euphemism for 'nearly drowned,' in the pitch black rivers of the Void and I was wet to the skin with Void water. When I had tried to go through the gate, it hadn't recognized me and sought to keep me out. Which meant trying to burn the skin from my bones. Since I had just experienced the literal burning of my skin from my bones, I wasn't too worried about the gate. Maybe it would recognise me, maybe it wouldn't, but I knew how to handle it now.

I took a few quick steps and then launched myself through the opening. It stung momentarily, then became a beautiful warm hug of energy. Evidently, the gate recognized me. Phew.

I needed to wake the gargoyles up and explain to them what had happened before they got a look at me. I made sure my hood was secure and that my face was in shadow.

They were going to freak out.

They were as I'd left them. Sitting sentinel on either side of my entryway. I walked up the steps and then sat down on one of the stone knee walls that framed the doorway.

"Guys?" I whispered, "I'm back."

The gargoyles twitched. It was very subtle, and if I hadn't been watching them so closely, I probably would have missed it. A little shimmer went up their backs, and Grog's ears wiggled.

"I'm alone. You can show yourselves."

More shimmering and a bit of shaking from Brog. It was cute watching their little stone butts wiggle; from behind, they looked like Bulldogs.

"Come along, gentlemen, it's time to get up. I need to talk to you."

Grog's body gave an almighty shake, and suddenly he was fully alive and scuttling towards me. He stopped short when he got a few feet away and peered at me. Soon his slightly slower brother, Brog, who had a sizeable chunk of stone missing from the side of his head, was also awake. Brog got down from his ledge and crawled across the entryway and up the other side to sit next to his brother. The two sat side by side as much as the ledge would allow and stared at me.

"Okay, so I look really bad," I said.

They were silent. I continued.

"Annnnd, it will look a lot worse when I pull back this hood. So I want you to prepare yourselves."

"What happened to you, my lady?" Grog's voice was barely a whisper.

"Well, I was attacked and almost killed, and as a defence mechanism, my body went into burn up mode. I didn't know this was possible, but apparently my species can, under extreme stress, burst into flames, explode really, and regenerate. That's where I've been the last few days, regenerating with another of my kind. It looks terrible, but I will be okay. And in a few weeks I'll probably have skin again..."

"You don't have any skin?" Brog cut in.

"No," I sighed, "I don't. I am just muscle over bone, which is actually a step forward. Yesterday I was just sinew over bone, so progress and stuff."

"Please show us." If it was possible for a stone to look pale, Grog was doing it.

"Okay."

I pulled back the hood just as the sun peeked out from behind a cloud and stabbed at my eyes. My newly minted lids couldn't really handle it, and I recoiled into the shadows on the stoop. Which really did nothing to reassure the two gargoyles before me, who screamed.

"Guys! Guys! It's okay! Sorry, I got the sun in my eyes. I'm okay." I sat in the shade and beckoned them forward. "Come closer, it's okay. Take a good look, and maybe it'll be less scary."

Brog was still breathing hard, but Grog had calmed down enough to take his hand and pull him along the ledge towards me. Grog gently placed a stone claw on my wrapped hand and peered into my face.

"Your eyes are the same." He turned to Brog. "Look, Brog, she is the same inside."

Grog wrapped his arm of stone around his brother and held him tight while the little gargoyle looked deep into my eyes. I tried not to smile too much because without skin it just doesn't work. I let my deep affection for this rocky house gargoyle shine through my eyes. Brog stepped forward, out of his brother's embrace and drew himself to his full height which placed us directly eye to eye. He was inches from my face, I could feel his breath, cool like a spring wind, against my raw cheek. He reached out a single claw-tipped finger and touched the tip of my nose.

"Boop," I whispered. Brog giggled, it sounded like rocks jangling around in a mason jar.

"You're still you," he smiled. "She's still her, Grog!"

"I know, Brog." A single pebble dropped from Grog's eye as he climbed down to the stoop. "Welcome home, Lady." With a little skip and a jump he had his hands on the front door latch and was swinging it open.

"Thank you, Grog." I walked through, Brog tight on my heels. "Grog, could you please take this sword through to the greenhouse?" I held out the bundle and Brog ferried it over to his brother as Grog swung around the door, his momentum pulling it closed.

"Oh course, my lady. Would you like it placed in the circle?"

"Always a step ahead of me, Grog. Yes, please. I'm hoping I can make some skin over these muscles."

"You have healed your wounds there before, this is no different."

"That's the plan. But first I need to get out of these sheets. Brog, can you come give me a hand?"

"Of course, my lady!"

He was halfway up the stairs before I put a foot on the first step.

18

Brog was so excited he chatted all the way up the stairs.

"And then there was this squirrel! He came around all the time, and he tried to hide some nuts under Grog, and I said we should scare the squirrel away, but Grog said no, and then the squirrel put one too many nuts under Grog, and he got real mad and growled at the squirrel and it ran away! I laughed so hard I fell off the stoop and Grog had to pick nuts out of his butt!"

"That's funny, Brog," I laughed. "I can just see Grog picking nuts out of his butt."

"I know! It was hilarious!" Brog did a somersault along the hallway. "What did you do while you were gone, lady?"

I'd tried several times to get them to call me Phoenix, they weren't into it, so I let it go.

"I told you, Brog," I said quietly, "I had an accident, and I was healing."

He stopped rolling down the hall and looked at me.

"Oh, yes, I forgot. You're still the same."

"Thank you, Brog, but I don't really feel the same."

It was the first time I'd said that out loud, and until that exact moment, I hadn't even considered it. No, I didn't feel the same. I felt exposed. I felt raw. I felt violated. I felt abandoned, even though I hadn't been. There were a lot of feelings I hadn't considered until this hushed moment with the very unassuming gargoyle.

"We're here!"

Brog plowed on, unaware of my introspection. Being around his energy was nice. Sure, he could be a little exasperating, but Brog's enthusiasm and love were genuine.

"Excellent."

And it truly was. My room was exactly how I'd left it: giant four-poster bed, long wall of mullioned windows, wall to wall closets and deep shag carpet that you could really sink into. Man, I had missed my room. I walked over to the wall of closets, their mirrored doors reflecting my fabric wrapped frame back at me in stunning detail. Wow, I looked like crap. The fabric strips were already starting to fray, and there was dirt all over my backside from where I'd sat on the stoop. My bloody looking head poking out of the top of it all was not helping the ensemble. And my wings, my poor wings, looked like a third grader's paper mache project. I need out of this crap and down to the garden.

"Time to get out of this stuff."

I tugged at a piece of cloth on my torso, trying to find an edge. I couldn't remember whether the strips were short pieces or one long sash I'd have to spin out of. I pulled on the fabric, and a loop came free, I tugged some more and felt something squelch on the opposite side of my stomach. Abandoning the torso, I went up to the neck and tried to loosen something there. Even with the open edge, it was no help. I wished I'd paid more attention when Royal was wrapping me.

I pulled harder on my neck. Things loosened but didn't come free. I grabbed at my arms, but they were wrapped tight, and my cloth-covered fingers weren't able to dig through the layers. What had they done to me? As an act of desperation, I chewed on the cloth near my wrist and yanked the fabric from my fingers.

I was breathing hard. Panic was everywhere. I looked up into the mirror and saw myself chewing on the cloth, my raw hand partly exposed; blood had welled up on my torso and around my neck. My eyes were bright and wide and spun around grotesquely in my muscle covered face.

I froze.

I stared at myself in the glass.

Then I fainted.

Not like the Travelling faints I used to get, just an old-fashioned I'm hyperventilating, and my life is too much faint. I woke up crumpled on the floor. I'd only been out for a moment. Brog was stroking my shoulder. It took me a moment to work out what he was saying.

"Don't worry, lady," his voice was barely above a whisper, "I will help you."

His little stony hands made quick but delicate work of the strips of cloth. With one hand he held the fabric away from my frame as the other sliced it cleanly with his sharp claws. When he had a few ends cut, he peeled them away from my body. I shifted on the ground as he tugged and quick as a bunny, well gargoyle, he had a pillow under my head and me laid out on my back.

"Just lie still," he smiled, "I can handle this."

At that moment I got a glimpse into who Brog had been before he got that chip in his head. Calm and gentle. Like a softer version of Grog. I knew the gargoyles were bonded pair, but as Brog gently tugged and pulled at my wrappings,

I realised just what a companion Brog was to Grog. Yes, now Grog was the primary caregiver, the big brother if you will, but there was a time when that responsibility was shared mutually between them. It made me sad to think of what Brog had lost, and the salty tears stung my eyes.

I didn't realize I was sobbing until Brog crawled over to my head and dabbed at my tears with a scrap of cloth.

"I'll be over soon, lady," his cool fingers were a blessing on my raw face. "Try to breathe." He put a hand on my cloth covered sternum and closed his eyes. "Peace," he whispered and a small warm pulse flowed around my heart. It was calm and clear and reminded me I was loved.

"Brog, I didn't know you could do that."

"I can do lots of things." He smiled, his voice taking on some of its natural buoyancy. I smiled. "Oh, good! You're happy again!" He sat back on his heels. "That means I can work much faster."

He giggled as he crawled down to my feet. Working faster was not an understatement. He moved up my legs with speed and precision. He was so quick with his little claws that the motion of pull and snip began to tickle. Soon I was laughing out loud as the little guy freed me from my fabric cage.

"Oh, lady," he said when he finished, "you don't look so good." He looked a bit scared. "But don't worry, you'll get better." I moved to sit up, but he stopped me. "Please don't get sad again."

"I'm okay now, Brog," I took his tiny clawed hand in mine. "Thank you for your help."

I didn't think stone could blush, but there it was. Brog cheeks reddened as he shuffled back so I would have room to get up.

I rolled on my side in the pile of used bandages, which

was about as gross as it sounds, and slowly moved to standing. I looked at myself in the full mirror, every inch of my raw glory in front of me. My breath sped up again, and Brog placed a hand on my leg.

"Go to your garden, lady."

19

———

I met Grog at the door to the greenhouse. When he saw me, he gasped but quickly recovered. I wanted to say something, but I was emotionally exhausted from what I'd gone through upstairs, and the look on Grog's face told me that words weren't necessary.

Grog grasped the handle of the enormous door in both hands and swung it open. A wave of warm moist air drifted over my exposed flesh. Grog bowed deeply to me as I stepped inside the greenhouse.

It was darker inside than I expected. I looked up to the glass ceiling and discovered giant black clouds had rolled in while I was upstairs getting unwrapped. I thought briefly of Sid and Spin sitting in the forest, but decided they could fend for themselves. I needed to focus on me right now.

The inky clouds above shrouded the greenhouse in an eerie greyness that threatened to rob the foliage of its power. I walked along the path, the soft grass floor coming up to meet my feet with every step. I ran my hands along the plants as I walked, and I felt the room awaken. With every step, the green of the trees and plants deepened.

As I arrived at the mouth of the healing circle a crack of lightning filled the sky. The energy of it sang through my body and out into the plants. We both stood a little taller.

Grog has placed the sword at the mouth of the circle. It was still tightly wrapped, but there was no mistaking its form as it lay in the twilight of the greenhouse. I stepped over the blade and felt a shimmer of power deep in my body. I needed this. I needed to be here. To heal.

And then I needed Archer.

I stepped into the circle.

The moment my exposed toes touched the soft soil of the circle, a giant crash of thunder filled my ears. The glass roof shook with the sheer weight of the sound. I walked to the middle of the circle and slowly looked around. The trees were as lush and as vibrant as I remembered, but the last time I had been here, it had been about brightness and warmth. Now it was about regeneration and blood.

This was not an act for sunlight.

Torrential rains made a sharp staccato on the roof, and more lightning shot across the sky. Thunder came soon after. I looked up and longed for the rain to wash down over me, to calm and repair me. As the thought formed in my mind, the sound of grinding gears filled my ears, and soon the great panels of the roof were being pulled back by some unseen machinery that knew the beat of my heart. As the roof opened, the rain poured in. It ran down my body and into the grass at my feet. I felt the trees and shrubs around me, the flowers, all reach a little higher towards the sky.

Suddenly a huge streak of lightning crackled across the sky and down into the greenhouse. It hit the ground a few feet away from me and bathed the circle in bright blue light. It formed a web of light around me, engulfing me as it created a perfect circle. I felt the energy of the greenhouse rush towards the lightning formed orb and infuse it with its power. The two sources melted into one and flowed around me in large washes of colour. Blue and green swirled before my eyes. I reached out my hands to the orb, my fingers brushing the surface, and the power locked on to me.

It filled me. I could feel the light move through my flesh. It coated every muscle; it strengthened every bone. The power pulled me off my feet, and I floated in the air. It caressed my wings, the fine muscles and tiny bones growing and stretching under its tutelage. I felt my wings grow.

And finally, I felt my power answer the call.

The part of me that had been dormant through this entire ordeal, the part of me that had just started my heart beating again, awoke with a cry that tore through my body and brought a soundless scream to my mouth. My back arched as it awakened. Every muscle in my body writhed as the power of the elements, and my own elemental power joined forces to heal my damaged flesh. But they could only take my fragile form so far before it would break.

Patches of darkness flashed before my eyes, and everything spun. I cried out to the powers to release me, to let me go before I broke apart. At first, they argued. The power of the storm wanted to push me further, but my power took control. It broke my connection to the elements, sending me tumbling to the ground. In the distance, I could hear the roof closing.

As the rain dissipated the forest stepped in to absorb the excess water and warm the ground beneath me. I lay on the grass in the centre of the greenhouse, spent and slightly numb. My power coiled itself around my heart, which was beating stronger than before, and rested.

The clouds above parted and sunlight streamed down. I sat up and looked at my hands. They were shiny with new skin, my arms as well. I looked down at my body and saw that new skin now covered me. The new shiny skin of a healing burn.

"It's not perfect. But it'll work," I said to the trees.

I got to my feet and looked at my body. My torso was now sealed in shiny skin that slid slightly over the muscle when I touched it. My breasts had returned, somewhat deflated, but there was definitely fat over the muscle. My ass, however, had not returned to its former glory. Sure, there was skin, but none of the meatiness I longed for.

I ran my hands over my face and found that I had eyelashes and lips again. My skull was covered with skin and a fine layer of stubble. My wings were whole. Well, chicken wing, no sauce, whole. They were thick with muscle and covered in skin, but no feathers. Not even down.

I still had far to go, but at least now I was sealed against the elements.

I walked over to my sword and picked it up, shaking it free of the wrapping, so I was holding the naked handle. I brought the blade to my lips and laid a kiss on the shaft.

"Come find me, Archer."

The sword pulsed for a moment and then went dark. With the sword in one hand, I walked out of the greenhouse.

"I need a bath."

20

I found the two gargoyles upstairs in my room. When I walked in their eyes got so wide I worried the stones themselves would fall out onto the carpet. I didn't think it would be much trouble for them to pop them back in, but who wants the hassle?

"How do I look?" I spread my arms wide and did a little twirl.

"You look much better," Grog lied.

"You still look gross," Brog, the voice of truth.

"Brog!" Grog gave him a little push. "You're not supposed to say that!"

"It's okay," I walked towards the mirrors and took in my appearance. "I do look pretty gross, but I also look way better than I did before I got here. Hey, the bandages are gone. Thank you guys." I smiled at them in the glass. They smiled back, their tiny stone teeth looked so cute. What is happening to me?

"We do what we can," Grog bowed, Brog following a few seconds behind him.

"Thank you." I turned from the mirrors and headed towards the bathroom. "I really need to clean up before Archer gets here. Can you guys light the fire?"

"Can we?!" Brog was scrambling through the doorway like a happy puppy.

"Great, I need a bath."

My bathtub is amazing. Amazing. Bathing in the power of the full moon is cool, but soaking in my gigantic, almost a small pond bathtub was just what the doctor ordered. Wait, do Travellers even have doctors? Never mind.

As I filled the tub, the gargoyles set about making the fire, sitting in the flames while they stoked them. The fireplace threw out a lot of heat, and soon the bathroom was toasty warm, and the tub was filled. With a great sigh, I slipped down into the water and let my stubble covered head go right under. When I came up for air, Brog was sitting on the edge of the tub.

"What's up, Brog?"

"Are you okay, lady?"

"Much better, thank you for your help."

"You're welcome." His stony brow furrowed as he looked down at the water. "Please be careful in there."

"I will."

I flicked some bubbles at him; he giggled and ran back to the fireplace. He and Grog settled down among the flames and closed their eyes.

I lay back in the tub and breathed deeply for what felt like the first time in days. This tub was so much better than Royal's. I experimented with the lotions and potions, going for the creamiest things I could find to soothe my new skin.

I pulled a bottle from the side of the tub and poured a bit into my hand. It felt like lotion and smelt like honey. I rubbed some of it on to my arm and was instantly soothed. I squirted a bunch into the tub and then rubbed some over my head and face. I felt greasy and gorgeous, and I rested my head back on the edge of the tub and closed my eyes. I could feel sleep pulling at the edges of me, and I let it come.

21

Flames filled my vision. Bright green and red scorching waves. I turned my head to see where they were coming from, but they were everywhere. They were coming from me. My body was burning. I had moved beyond pain. It was so intense that my mind no longer registered it. I felt wrongly calm. Flames licked at me, but my arms hung limply at my sides. I peered through the flashes of green and red fire at the surrounding scene. I was in the Void. I could just make out one of the deep dark streams a short distance away.

Someone was screaming.

They were screaming my name. I listened harder, tried to turn towards the voice. As I strained my ears, it revealed more words. They were screaming for me to run towards the stream. They were screaming at me to douse the flames that covered me. They were trying to save me. But I didn't need saving. I didn't want saving.

Something in my heart shifted, and the flames turned to black. I was burning within my pain. My guilt. I had earned this. I had caused this. I would not burn like my people usually did. I would burn black and hard, and then I would be nothing. Then this immortal creature would be no more. Then the pain in my heart would cease, and I would be free of this crushing knowledge. I caused this. I made all this happen. It was my fault.

The voice was still screaming.

The black fire tore at my structure and sent me to my knees. I felt something pounding on the ground. My eyes were losing focus. Blackness clawed at my vision, deep black like the flames around me. The pounding continued. I looked up and saw a man a few feet away, pounding his fist on the ground. His shape was unclear. I could see his height and feel his power try to soothe the edges of my fire. But he was not strong enough. It was almost over. I lay down on the ground and accepted my fate. The man ran towards me, framed by the grey sky. He had wings.

22

———

My eyes snapped open. I was in the tub. The water was warm. Okay, I thought to myself; I haven't been out that long. Was that a dream or a vision? I wanted to say dream, but it had all the hallmarks of a vision. Crap. What was that all about? Obviously this was a sneak peek into another time I had burned. Interesting, I hadn't even thought of that, but it made sense. My former self was thousands of years old. I'd burned before.

"You're back."

The deep voice shook me from my thoughts and ripped a scream from my throat.

"Holy shit! Archer! You scared the hell out of me!"

"I was waiting for you to wake up."

Archer was sitting on the long plush bench that divided the bath area from the shower area. He was in his usual black leather pants and nothing else, which revealed his chiselled torso and sculpted arms. His face was open with high cheekbones and a square chin. His eyes were bright and clear as he focused on me and his hair was a long sheet of ebony that draped down to his waist. He was the picture of symmetry.

And every inch of his skin was silver.

"You're back." It wasn't a question.

"Yep." I've learned that Travellers like short, slightly cryptic answers.

"Where were you?" Archer was sitting casually, one leg draped over the other, leaning back, so his silver abs rippled just so. Wow. But he was holding himself very still. And I was very aware that only my head, arguably the least gruesome part of me, was poking out of the water.

"Another of my kind was taking care of me."

"What happened?"

"Apparently my kind can burst into flame and regenerate when under extreme stress." I shrugged, but the bath water only rippled. He nodded. We both knew what the 'extreme stress' was. "But I'm still not entirely healed."

"I can see that," his voice cracked. He still hadn't moved.

"The rest of me is worse, much worse." Archer nodded again, but this time a single silver tear slipped down his cheek. "Archer, I will get better. In fact, this is already much better. Seriously. I was just bone when I started, and now I have eyelashes." I tried to smile, but I could feel it pull at my flesh awkwardly and a slight shiver ran up Archer's body. He stood and stepped towards the tub.

"May I see you?" His shoulders were relaxed, but his hands were tight fists.

"Okay, just brace yourself." He nodded.

I stood up.

I tried to do it slowly, to kind of ease him into it, but the bottom of the tub was slippery from all the lotion, and my ultra-smooth feet slipped on the bottom. I had to rush to keep from toppling out of the tub. By the time I was upright, Archer's jaw was hanging open and slack in a way I'd never seen before.

"Are you okay?" I asked.

"Am I okay?" He shook his head, his ebony hair swayed. "You stand there looking like you've walked through fire and ask me if I'm okay?"

"Well, I did kind of walk through fire."

"And now jokes!" He reached for me and then stopped short, his hands clenching and unclenching in the air. "I thought you were dead! I thought Mhyr had killed you! When the orb of power exploded, I thought you were gone forever! I was right! Look at you! You did die. For only death could turn a person into this." His breath was coming in gasps, sobs soon followed. "I was so worried about you." He was weeping now. "I thought you were gone again."

He collapsed on the bench and put his head in his hands. I stepped carefully out of the tub and went to his side. The air in the bathroom was warm thanks to the gargoyles, and I wrapped my naked body around him and kissed him on the cheek.

"I'm so sorry," I whispered in his ear. "I should have let you know I was alive sooner, but I'd never experienced this before. I needed to understand what was happening before you could see me."

"Why? Did you think I couldn't handle this?"

"Those first few days, I looked," my voice caught in my throat, "I looked so horrible. I really didn't think I would heal. I didn't want anyone to see me so fragile. I needed to hate myself in peace."

Archer shifted on the bench to wrap his arms around me. He held me a little too tightly and kissed the top of my stubbly head, gently rocking me.

"I will always be there for you. I will never turn away from you. You can always count on me." He lifted my chin, so we were eye to eye. "I love you."

That's when I lost my shit.

Yep, bawled out all the pain and fear and stress of the last few days all over his large chiselled shiny silver chest. He held me through all of it, at one point pulling me onto his lap and cradling me in his arms like a giant hairless baby. Well, I guess babies are generally hairless, but I did not look cute nor was I soft, so maybe like a giant hairless rat? Anyway, it was a big feat considering my wings were also large flaps of flesh and bone at my back.

When I calmed down, I slid from his lap, and he draped my robe around me, helping me get my arms and my wings inside and then tying it snugly. He paused as he finished his knot, his brow furrowed as he looked over my shoulder.

"Why did you bring the gargoyles up here?" The last time Archer had registered their presence, I was rubbing their stone heads goodbye as we walked down my front steps.

"Oh, I wanted the company." He cocked an eyebrow. I tried a version of the truth. "Sometimes they move around the house when I'm not here."

"Right."

He bought that? There was so much I needed to learn about the Traveller world. Like, what happens in a person's life for them to readily accept stone statues that can move of their own volition?

"Are you hungry?" he asked as he towelled off his chest. His beautiful, chrome, chest.

"What?" Archer looked up and smiled with just a little heat in his eyes.

"I said," he moved the towel slowly, "are you hungry?"

"Yep," I nodded just as slowly, "very."
"Then let's get you something to eat."
He took my hand, and we went down to the kitchen.

23

———

Archer is a surprisingly good cook. And I had a surprisingly well-stocked kitchen. As I munched on scrambled eggs and toast, (where did I get toast? Who is bringing this magic toast to my house?), I filled Archer in on what Sid had said about us being let into the City of Caves.

"I agree."

"That was easy." Archer put more eggs on my plate, and I shovelled them down. "So you think Sid is right?"

"Yes, it all makes sense now. We passed through the gates far too easily."

"They had the two guards though."

"Ha!" his laugh was a sharp crack that reverberated around the kitchen. "They killed themselves before we even got close. And if they had not, we would have made quick work of them. No, the entrance itself was the challenge, and we sailed through it. Sid is on to something."

"Okay, if Sid is right, then who set us up?" More eggs, damn, regenerating really makes a woman hungry. "It had to be someone that knew Greldrom hadn't set the Bounty, knew who had set the Bounty, and was also powerful enough to break the charm on the gate. Or, and this is even scarier, was powerful enough to bargain with Big G himself and get him to open the gate."

"We need more information."

"Duh."

"Excuse me?" he looked genuinely puzzled.

"It's human for," I searched for it around mouthfuls of egg, "Duh."

"Very illuminating."

"There's something else we need to discuss." Archer just stared at me, his face perfectly blank. It's weird how good these Travellers get at hiding all emotion. "I've been asked to join the Guard."

"I am aware."

"And?"

"And, what?"

"And what are your thoughts on that?"

"It will not be easy for you. Although you are a powerful creature, you are new to your power and not yet confident in wielding it. There will be some on the Guard who will resent your position. You may technically have joined as the sole member of your race, but now you will be joining as the leader of the Minions. Effectively taking over two seats. It will not be met without opposition."

After I had figured out the double negatives, I had a few questions.

"But what about us?"

"Us?"

"Yes, us. The coupling and such. Is that something that will be a problem for the Guard?"

"I had not considered it."

He was silent for a long time.

"Well?" I asked.

"I am considering it. Yes. It will be a problem for them, and we should not make them aware of our relationship until you have firmly established yourself as an influential member of the Guard."

"Right," I picked at my few remaining eggs.

"You seem displeased by this."

"Of course I'm displeased! You're my boyfriend! And now we've got to keep that hidden. It doesn't feel good."

"Getting a knife in the back would feel worse."

"Wow. Just wow," I got up from the counter. "I'm going to get dressed now. When I'm ready, I'll be gathering Spin and Sid and heading to the City of Caves. I need to figure out what's going on there before I go meet the Guard. You're welcome to come along," I paused in the doorway, "If you think you can handle it."

"I will be fine."

"Sure."

I walked out, my newly formed face set to resting bitch. I was getting better at this.

24

————

Up in my bedroom, I opened all the closet doors and started working my way through. If history had taught me anything, it was that I had an appropriate outfit for every eventuality. I was sure my pre-human-world self had something fitting for my current weird shiny skin state.

I found it in the closet nearest the end. A dark grey jumpsuit with a deep hood and fabric envelopes for my wings. I pulled it from the closet and laid it out on the bed. This was going to be one complicated dressing situation. I closed the bedroom door and turned the lock. I hoped that Archer would stay downstairs and didn't have some kind of crazy supernatural hearing. Then I called to the gargoyles.

"Hey, guys?" I stepped into the bathroom; they sat frozen in the cooling embers of the fire. "I need your help with something." Still, they didn't move. "It's okay, I've locked the bedroom door, and Archer is downstairs. He won't see you."

At those words, Grog's stone ears twitched. Soon Brog's were wiggling. Within moments, they were both back to life and sitting at my feet.

"I need your help to get into this jumpsuit."

"It would be our pleasure," Grog intoned as he bowed deeply, dragging Brog down with him.

"Great. Let me just put on some underwear first."

Damn, it felt great to put on panties. Weird, yes, but I had been undergarment free for the past few days as I had no butt or breasts to deal with. Now that I was clipping myself into a bra and sliding on some full briefs, I was feeling whole again. Man, give me a handbag, and I'd feel positively put together.

The gargoyles looked bulky and stiff, but they could be agile and delicate in their movements. Brog was so good with the wing flaps that soon he was directing Grog on what to do. He was the one that figured out I needed to put on the pant legs and then sit on the bed so they could shift both my arms and wings into the upper half of the suit at the same time. Complicated, but the finished result was flattering.

I stood before the mirror as they each worked to lace me into the matching boots Brog had found at the back of the closet. He had also unearthed a matching sheath for my sword and two small holders for the blades I typically wore on my forearms. Those proved to be too much for my newly formed flesh though, so Grog adapted them to go over the boots so I could still carry the extra blades. I pulled up the hood and checked myself out in the glass.

"I look good."

"You do, my lady," Grog agreed.

"Until you take off the hood," Brog said seriously.

"Brog!" Grog shot the gargoyle a look.

"No, it's okay. Brog is right." I pulled back the hood. My face looked brutal, like a bunch of flesh colour plastic wrap pulled too tightly over a bowl of raw chicken; raw chicken that still had bits of feathers along the eyebrows and scattered around the head. "The effect is gruesome." I turned a bit to see my cauliflower ears. "Maybe I can use it to my advantage?"

"You can scare people with it!" Brog suggested.

"That's for sure," I pulled up the hood. "But for now I'll keep it hidden. I'm heading out for a while, I've got to go visit the minions and then see the Guard." The gargoyles' stony faces paled to a limestone grey. "I'll be okay guys. Those places are safe for me now." That could be true. You never know. "You guys can hang out up here after I'm gone if you'd like."

"Can we build a fire?" Brog asked.

"Sure." I smiled, based on the widening of the gargoyles' eyes, it wasn't quite the beatific face I thought it was. "Just keep an eye on it." I patted them both on the head and went downstairs.

I met Archer at the door. He had taken my sword and a few of my shorter blades and sharpened them in my weapon room. Yeah, I have one of those, but it isn't nearly as balls out as Archer's. He helped me slide the sword into the holster at my back and fit the shorter blades into my boot holsters.

"This is a great outfit," he commented as he slid the third blade home.

"Really? You think so?"

"Yes, very practical," he ran his hands over my waist, "And flattering."

"Thanks, baby," I pulled back my hood to kiss him. He hesitated for the tiniest of moments and then planted his lips on mine. Well, lips being the word I was using for the newly formed pieces of skin that were currently surrounding my mouth. I had a feeling it would take a while before they resembled conventional lips.

He brought the hood back up over my head and then opened my massive front door like it was a paper screen. Not going to lie, it was super-hot to see him just casually open the door that gave everyone else, including myself, so many problems. I took his hand in mine, and we walked out across the lawn. The door swung shut behind us with a gentle thud.

When we got to the gate, I released his hand. He looked sharply at me.

"We're keeping things a secret, remember?"

"Right."

25

Archer went through the gate before me. I took a moment to look back at the house. I needed to spend more time here. I was going on a serious staycation when all this was over. Sigh, it probably would never be over. I'd only been a Traveller for a few months and every day seemed to bring with it more drama and more mystery. I hadn't even had time to consider the vision I'd had in the tub. Who was the guy with the wings? And black flames? What the hell was that about? I shook my head like a minion and stepped through the gate.

I needn't have worried about Sid and Spin during the storm. They had fashioned quite the little camp site for themselves. In the relatively brief time I'd been inside, these two had a sturdy shelter built and a fire blazing. And what looked like two squirrels cooking over the flame.

"Wow, you guys know how to settle in," I said.

Spin smiled when he saw me.

"Oh, lady, you look much better," he wiped his hand on a cloth he'd gotten from somewhere. "And that outfit is very fitting."

"Thank you, Spin," I gestured at the campsite. "Thought I'd be gone a while, eh?"

"Well, when the rains started Sid suggested we build a shelter, and you can't have a shelter without a fire, and you can't have a fire without food!" He pulled one of the meat sticks from the flame. "Squirrel?"

"Don't mind if I do," Archer sat down on a rock and tore into the flesh.

"I'm good, thanks."

"May we see your face?"

It was the first thing Sid had said since we'd joined them. I pulled back my hood.

"What do you think?" I asked.

Sid crawled out from under the shelter. I sat down next to Archer so he could get a closer look. Sid stood up and walked around me slowly.

"Remarkable," he whispered, "remarkable."

"I look good, right?"

"My lady, when I first saw you I did not understand how you would heal, let alone if it could be done. In fact, I can confess it now, I had my doubts that you would ever be whole again. But after one healing session, you have brought yourself to this state. It is promising. Do you look good? No. You do not. You do however appear to be healing. And that is all we can ask for." He stepped back and cocked his head to the side. "I wish your hair would grow back faster."

"You and me both," I pulled my hood back up. "Now, before we go to the Caves, I need you guys to fill me in on what has been happening there."

The minions just stood there. Neither said a word.

"Guys, this is where you talk and tell me what has been happening in the Caves."

The minions slowly turned their heads, looked at each other, then looked back at me. Spin spoke.

"It is best you see for yourself."

"Oh, that sounds great." Sarcasm, best friend of every tough girl.

Travelling with two minions and a, hmm, I don't know what Archer's people called themselves; let's go with 'silver dudes'... Travelling with two minions and a silver dude, two of whom think they're in charge, was interesting. What was even more interesting was watching Sid and Archer figure out how to hold hands in the manliest way possible. Since Sid and Spin knew how to get to the City of Caves, they need to be in control. Since they were on the small side, they each needed to take one of us. Spin quickly took my hand as Sid had explained this, I think he feared Archer.

We bounced and bumped into each other as we moved through the Time Tunnel but landed on our feet. The last time Archer and I had been here, we'd arrived further back from the canyon. This time we ended up right before the enormous cauldron that guarded the entrance to the City of Caves. It was night again. Was it always night here? The only light coming from the stars up above.

"Why is the fire out?" I asked. No one answered. "And why are the torches out?"

I looked at Sid and Spin. Spin was pale, minion pale. A light sheen of sweat had formed on his upper lip despite the chilly desert night. Sid's face had gone blank; whatever emotions he felt trapped deep in his heart.

"You guys are freaking me out. Snap out of it."

I snapped my fingers in front of Sid's face; his hand shot out and grabbed my wrist.

"Do not do that."

"Sorry," I pulled my hand away, "But you guys need to tell me what's going on."

"The minions are violent creatures," Spin sounded far away as his voice filled the darkness. "You saw the atrocities that were taking place the last time you were here."

"I did."

"As the humans say, that was the tip of the iceberg. I cannot remember a time when our people did not engage in violence for sport."

"Remember the Colosseum?" Sid asked. I didn't like the smile on his face.

"Of course I do," Spin snapped. "We have always been violent and power hungry. When you took the head of Greldrom, you became our leader, but just as quickly you were gone. And into that space crawled the most power hungry, the most violent of us. The ones that sat simpering at Greldrom's side, all the while waiting for his downfall." Spin turned to me. "There have been battles for succession. They began almost immediately. Inside those caves are hundreds of minions, all scrambling for position, all unsure of what will come next, unsure of who will rule."

"This all went down in a couple days?" I asked.

"This has been going on for centuries," Sid said.

"When you walk through that gate you must take for your rightful place as leader of our kind," Spin said.

"They will fight you," Sid said.

"And you will win!" Spin countered.

"Shit, guys! Why didn't you tell me all this back at the house?" I thought about my single sword and small blades. "I would have brought more firepower."

"I'm always packing." Archer drew from the scabbard on his back one of, okay, the biggest sword I'd ever seen.

"Damn!" I said. Archer's eyes shone in the darkness. "Are you going to be okay in there? No freaking out?" His eyes flicked quickly to the two minions before answering.

"I will be fine. I cannot sense the same darkness that was here before." He took a deep breath like he was scenting the air. "This is just violence. More chaotic, but not the soul dampening darkness of before."

"Oh man, we're doing this aren't we?"

Spin touched my hand.

"Remember my pain, my lady? Remember what I showed you?"

"I do."

When I'd first moved through the caves, Spin had been my guide. My vision power had picked up on some of his experiences down in the throne room, and they were not cool. Seriously messed up shit. I had vowed then that I would put a stop to the pain and bloodlust that Greldrom had been spreading. And now it was time to make good on that promise.

I pulled my sword from my back and looked at the blade. It pulsed a red warning in my hands.

"No violence." I put the sword away. "We offer no violence until we receive it." I looked at Archer. "Put your sword away. We will use our power to get down to the throne room."

"You're serious?" he asked.

"You are a member of the Guard," I placed a hand on his beautiful silver shoulder. "One of the most powerful creatures in the Void," I ran my hand down his arm until we were both holding the hilt of his sword. My power flared. I felt it move from our joined hands through my veins. I felt my wings spread and my spine straighten. These were my people. I was their ruler. I would protect them. I would decide for them. They would be mine.

"Let us do this as kings would."

Archer put up his sword and fell into step behind me as I walked into the City of Caves.

26

———

There was no heavy shift of power or spell of darkness blocking the entry. We just walked through, which put a real dent in my strut. But I shrugged it off and clung to the power I had called before we entered the Caves. It was cold in here, the night breezes of the canyon picking up speed at the entrance and whipping ahead of us down the passage. Some torches were lit, and some had been ripped from the walls.

I heard Sid shuffle up beside me.

"They are all in the throne room."

"How do you know that?" I asked.

"I can feel them."

"And now would be a splendid time to remind you we are rebuilding our friendship and keeping any information from me would be very bad."

"My lady," he said the word as sarcastically as a dignified minion could, "save it for the enemy."

"Could you two focus, please?" Archer's voice was a deep bass that rolled through me even when my power wasn't on high alert.

"Got it." I kept my gaze forward, waiting for something to jump out at me. "Spin, where do you feel the others?" A few beats of silence. "Spin?"

"I can't."

"You can't what?"

"I can't feel them, my lady."

"What?" I stopped short and turned to him. Archer quickly moved in front of me to watch the passage. "What do you mean you can't feel them?"

"I reach out," he closed his eyes and literally reached into the air, it shimmered slightly. "But I cannot find them."

"Is that bad?" I asked Sid.

"It isn't good," he said calmly.

"Damn. Okay, Spin," I put one hand on his shoulder. "Stay close to me, and Arc..." I remembered the names Travel and bit my tongue. "Keep an eye on him if stuff gets hairy. Okay?" Archer nodded.

Spin would have attached himself to my leg like one of my blades if I'd let him. He settled for being close enough that I kicked him every other step.

The Minions designed the tunnels to mess with your mind. They sloped slowly downward and moved back and forth so you could never be sure just which direction you were going. Or from which direction the enemy could be coming. Archer stayed in the lead, which I was grateful for. He had put his blade away but was one of the quickest draws I'd ever seen. Okay, okay, I haven't seen many swords drawn. All right, zero swords drawn. But take my word for it, the man is fast. When he needs to be. Wink, wink. Too much? Okay, back to the tunnel.

We had been going for what felt like hours but was only minutes, when the air took on a strange odour.

"Do you guys smell that?" I asked.

"Of course," Archer responded.

"What is it?"

"Death." Sid's answer was a bit too quick for my liking.

"Death?"

"Death and blood and piss and sweat and tears."

"Party time," I said.

"Exactly," Sid replied.

"Sid, I was being sarcastic."

"So was I."

He didn't sound sarcastic. I had a feeling there was more to Sid than I knew. His taste in fun was far more 'minion' than I had previously realised.

Archer froze. I didn't see it happening. My eyes were on Sid, but I felt it. I felt it deep in the pit of my stomach.

Time slowed down, and I turned towards Archer just as he drew his sword. I dropped to a crouch and shoved Spin back against the wall. Sid scuttled out of my peripheral vision. I heard Spin grunt as he hit the wall, and then the wave of minions rounded the corner.

Time sped back up to real life speed as thirty minions bore down on us. Archer stepped back onto his right leg and pulled back his sword, preparing to sweep across the first row of attackers. Before his blade could swing, I stepped forward and hooked my arm under his.

"No violence!"

He pulled against my arm, the shadow of bloodlust appearing at the edges of his eyes. I thrust my free arm forward towards the oncoming minions and called forth my power.

It had never worked that fast. The space between thought and action was virtually non-existent. A large glob of bright blue power shot from my hand and hit the crowd of minions head on. It splattered across them, covering the first few rows in blue goo. Those minions struck by the goo dropped like rocks to the floor, their little chests moving up and down quickly. The rest kept coming.

"Crap," I whispered.

"Exactly," Archer said.

He shoved me off and stepped forward, swinging his sword left and right. Minions were falling like leaves, and still Archer kept swinging. Soon splatters of blue, green and purple covered the walls. Minion blood.

I heard Spin sob, and something in me broke free.

"Stop," I said the word quietly. Softly. "Stop." A little louder this time, almost above the sounds of violence. "Stop!"

I screamed the word, and my power screamed with it.

Bright green lightning jumped from my hands, ripping apart my gloves and exposing my raw, tight skin. My hood flew back, revealing my stretched skin and grotesque mouth. I screamed the word again, and my power blasted through the tunnel like a tornado. It swirled around the minions, forcing them to the ground. I tugged at the collar of my suit to reveal my sternum. It pulsed with green light. I walked towards the minions that had attacked us, and they scattered for the walls.

"Stop." Everyone froze. "There will be no more of this." They all just stared. "Answer me." My words were calm. If I hadn't been trying to save our lives, I would have found it creepy. "Tell me this uprising is over."

The minions answered in unison.

"It is over, my lady."

"Good, very good. Now walk with me. It is time to take my throne." I took a step forward, then stopped. "Archer, Spin, Sid, join me."

The three men took positions behind me like a gnarly group of bodyguards. I started walking.

"My lady?" Spin was at my heel again.

"Yes, Spin?"

"Your hair has come back."

I dragged my hand across my skull, and yes, my hair had grown back. It was only about an inch long, but that was significantly better than it had been even an hour ago.

"Well, isn't that awesome?"

"It is, my lady."

Archer's voice cut across the tunnel.

"What is the plan?"

"To take back my throne," I answered.

"They know you are coming," Sid said.

"Good."

27

My strut was on fleek (did I say that right?) by the time we reached the throne room. At one point, Spin told me I was humming; I had inadvertently started singing my own theme song. Bah, bah, bah! Anyway... I was strutting, and the minions we had overcome in the passageway were now moving in formation behind me, their shuffling steps sounding in unison.

I could hear the din of the throne room up ahead. It sounded chaotic. I stopped. The minions behind me stopped. I looked back at them; they stared at me.

"Who here can tell me what is happening right now in the throne room?" I asked the group.

"I can, my lady." A large minion stepped forward, well by minion standards he was large. He had a good fifteen to twenty pounds on Sid and was at least three inches taller. A massive minion.

"What is your name?"

"I am called Thunk."

"Fitting. What can you tell me, Thunk?"

"There have been skirmishes. Two distinct factions are vying for leader. They are both bloodthirsty."

"So I must defeat them both," I said. It was not a question.

"You have already defeated one, my lady."

"You?" I raised my eyebrows. "You led one faction?"

"I did."

"And you no longer oppose me?"

"No, I do not."

"And now you welcome my leadership?"

"Oh, no, my lady. I despise you." He said the words calmly, with only a hint of malice behind his eyes. "You are not one of us, and you never will be. But you have bested me. And you did it easily. I must carry that shame and agree to your superiority." He bowed deeply. "You are our leader." The 'for now' hung silently in the passageway.

"Glad you've come to your senses." I addressed the group at large. "I will need your help to retake the throne, but we will do it without violence." I could feel their silent protest. "There will be no violence! Things here have been twisted and dark for too long. It is time for free air to move through these caves."

I turned back to the passage, stretching out my arms and my wings as wide as they would go. I breathed in deeply and my lungs filled with the stink of sweat and blood and fear. My heart ached with it, and the orb of power that lived deep in my body throbbed in anger and sadness. This was not a world for me. But it was not a world I would turn from. These creatures, these minions, would be offered my protection; I would coat the walls of this place with my power until I purged every last one of them of the darkness that swirled here.

I breathed this in and when I exhaled, a stream of power

burst from my mouth like a gale. My power blew down the passage before me, and I followed it, moving down the hall with my arms and wings stretched to brace myself against the strength of power that sprang from my body.

I rounded a corner and saw the entrance to the throne room. I inhaled again, and my power pulled back and then doubled down as I exhaled. The strong wind swirled through the entrance with me right behind it, my entourage at my back. I was vaguely aware of Spin's hand clinging to my leg as I walked. I closed my mouth and watched as my power moved through the massive room.

It looked much like it did the last time I was in this place. There were minions everywhere; even hanging from the walls. Instinctually, I gestured towards them, and their shackles opened. They slid gently down the walls, cradled by my power. The wind ripped through the room, picking up the most violent minions and pinning them to the walls.

The throne was before me. A minion clung to it as a swirling column of my power pulled at him. I took the few steps up to the throne in a single stride, my wings, for the first time in weeks, flapping to boost my ascent. I stepped right up to the creature. His little fingers were digging into the filthy arms of the throne. I looked at him, and his eyes widened. I bent down and blew a slow stream of power into his hands. His fingers turned icy blue as his hands slipped from the throne. He flew across the room and was pinned against the wall with his brethren.

I turned to the room. My entourage spread out around me. Archer moved to stand just behind the throne; Sid found a place on the steps. The minions from the tunnel fanned out on the floor before me. Spin stood close to me, his hand resting on the throne itself. Some remaining minions crouched on the ground, holding wounded limbs and cowering. Others stared from their place on the walls, a look of anger and awe on their faces.

I took my seat on the throne.

"I have returned to claim my place as your leader," I scanned the crowd. "I offer you no violence and promise you no oppression. I am here to change things. I am here to make sure the weak are cared for, and the strong are generous. I am here to stop the pain and scrub the darkness from these walls."

"And we welcome you, my lady." A minion crouching on the floor, but unhurt, had spoken.

"I remember you."

"Yes, my lady." He stood. "I knew you would return."

It was Rogmesh, the one who had helped me take charge of things after I had beheaded Greldrom.

"I see things here have gotten a bit out of hand."

"Yes, my lady." He stepped forward. "There has been great unrest these past few days, but now that you are back we can breathe easy again."

"Traitor!" A voice screamed from the wall. "How dare you side with this bird! She is not one of us!"

"Silence!" Rogmesh yelled. "You show some respect!"

The yelling minion spat an enormous chunk of phlegm in my direction. I mean huge. Disgusting, but impressive.

"There's your respect."

"Bastard!" Rogmesh cried, he moved to run at the wall minion.

"Enough!" My voice filled the room. "Enough. Thank you, Rogmesh, but we will have no more violence."

"Yes, my lady," he stepped back. "But what will we do with him and his conspirators?"

"Give me a second," I gestured to Sid, Spin and Archer. They huddled close. "Guys, what should we do with them?"

"Kill them." I could always count Archer on for the prag-matic response.

"No, Archer."

"You could put them in the jails," Spin offered.

"You guys have jails?" I asked.

"Oh, yes," Sid said. "They are built much deeper in the rock."

"Are they big enough to hold all these guys?"

"Definitely. They're huge," Spin said.

"Okay, but then what?" I asked the men.

"Then what, what?" Archer asked.

"Then what do we do with them?" They all stared at me. "No one has any ideas?" More stares. "Okay, we'll put them in the jails for now." I rubbed my now beginning-to-throb head.

"Your hair's grown again," Spin whispered as the boys stepped back.

"All those against me will be placed in the jails," I called out to the room. There was a bit of murmuring from the group. "We will care for them, they will have food, water and bedding."

"You're too soft to handle us, bird!" Wall minion yelled.

"Rogmesh," I pointed to wall minion. "Take him first."

"Yes, Ma'am," Rogmesh smiled.

I pulled my hood up and sank back into my throne.

28

Getting all the opposing minions down to the jails took a while. It was also super uncomfortable to watch. Each one of them had their own special way of making it difficult for the minions on my side to grab them and take them away. Some went limp, others just let rip long streams of expletives; including quite a few I hadn't heard before and noted for future use.

Mr Wall minion stayed in his wheelhouse and hocked wads of phlegm at everyone from the moment they peeled him off the wall to the moment they locked him in his cell. The minions' flaky skin mixed with the phlegm to form a kind of paste that took two additional minions and a damp cloth to remove. I gagged hard a few times while they were cleaning it off. Not very leader-ish, but it was truly disgusting.

By the time they had deposited all those who opposed my rule in the cells, the minions were toast, and I was emotionally exhausted. Spin took my hand and spoke to me quietly.

"My lady," he asked, "Do you know some people who could help you with all this?"

"Hmm?" I wasn't quite in a sentence forming state of mind.

"Do you know some other Travellers who could advise you and work with you to manage all of this? Rogmesh can handle things here for you, but if you are going to join the Guard, you will need a council to help you navigate what is happening."

"Spin makes an excellent point," Archer's voice was clear and cold. Evidently, the dragging of various secreting minions down to the cells had not fazed him. "What about the siren and misshapen man that were with you in the Circle?"

"The man is Benyst," Sid said as he drew closer, his voice low. "He is a powerful creature. He would be a significant asset. And the siren is called Noiryn. She is not as powerful, but she is loyal."

"Noiryn is more powerful than she lets on," I said. "She saved me in the forest after Baba Yaga attacked."

I didn't tell them about the vision I had of Noiryn pulling me from the ocean when I had tried to kill myself. I hadn't even discussed that with her. Maybe it was time I did.

"Spin, you're right. I could use more firepower going into this meeting, especially as Archer can't stand with us."

"He can't?" Sid asked, but there was a hint of contempt there.

"It will be better for Phoenix if the Guard is unaware of our friendship."

"Oh," Spin said. Sid was silent.

"Archer's right." The F word hurt me, but I understood why he used it. "It will call into question some of my earlier activities, and I so do not need that right now." I stood up.

"Rogmesh?" I called, he was giving instructions to a group of minions, "can you come here, please?"

"My lady," he dropped to hands and feet and was beside me in seconds. "How may I be of service?"

"For starters, just call me Phoenix." His eyes widened. "Seriously. The 'my lady' stuff is feeling a bit suffocating." I turned to Sid and Spin. "That goes for you two as well. I think after today the Names will have Travelled all over the place."

"Indeed," Sid said. I turned back to Rogmesh.

"I need to get out of here for a little while, well, maybe a long while. I have a couple people to see, and then I have to go visit the Guard."

"And take your rightful place as our leader," he said proudly.

"Well, I'm not sure it'll be as easy that, but hope is free." Archer snorted, I shot him a look. "I'm trying to sound like a leader over here." I turned back to Rogmesh. "So, I will leave you in charge while I'm gone. Are you okay with that?"

"Of course, my.." he gulped, "Phoenix." He said the word slowly, like it might hurt his tongue. "I would be happy to lead in your absence."

"Good, now we need a way for you to get in touch with me if things get crazy here. Archer? Any ideas on that?"

"There is the Call." I waited for him to continue, but he said nothing.

"And how does one do the Call?" I will not get annoyed. I will not get annoyed. I will not...

"You do not know?" he asked.

I counted to a million; okay, three.

"No, I don't. I'm coming from the human world, remember?"

"Oh yes, sorry," he stepped forward. "Each of you, give me a hand."

"You're not going to explain it?" I asked.

"It will be faster if I just do it," he replied.

"Right." I gave him my hand; Archer looked at the shredded bits of glove and frowned. "Just rip it off," I said.

He did, exposing more of my weird shiny hand. Rogmesh coughed out a small shocked sound, but quickly recovered and placed his little flaky hand into Archer's open silver palm.

Archer took our two hands and pressed the palms together. He held them tightly with one hand and then, before I could protest, quickly drew a rib from his torso and drove it through both our hands. Rogmesh and I screamed and tried to pull away, but Archer held us fast. The rib bone vibrated, and Archer whispered as sharp currents of power shot from the bone and through our palms. I could feel Rogmesh's pulse against my hand, and I was sure he could feel mine. Our heart beats raced each other, who would be faster, who would control the pulse.

"Be in your power, Phoenix," Archer said. "You are the leader."

I told my heart to be calm, to relax, I told Rogmesh's heart to follow mine, to let me lead. It took a few deep breaths, but soon our hearts were beating in unison. When we had both steadied our breathing, the bone wiggled like it was trying to work free of our hands. Archer reached out and took the tip of his rib between his fingers and with a quiet word, pulled it free. It was back inside his torso before Rogmesh's, and my hand had separated.

"What the hell was that?" I asked, holding my hand to my chest.

"You are welcome," Archer said. "You can now contact

Rogmesh whenever you need to, and he can do the same." He stared hard at Rogmesh. "But only when it is necessary."

"Yes, sir," Rogmesh said.

"You just shoved a freaking bone through our hands!"

"Yes, that is how it works."

"You're supposed to tell people what's happening before you make an enormous hole in their hands!"

"Your hands are fine."

I looked down at my hand. It was fine. There wasn't even a mark where the bone had gone through.

"Are you okay, Rogmesh?"

"Yes, Phoenix."

"Then I guess we'd better get going." I stepped off the dais and headed out of the throne room. "My life is so weird," I said to no one in particular.

29
———

It was night when we arrived at Benyst's house; I have never seen daylight here. We landed in the circle of grass, the stars a beautiful glowing blanket above us. I loved this place. This was where I had reattached my first wing and made my first attempts at flight. It hadn't amounted to more than a few big hops, but it had been way cool.

I took in the circle of torches, the lush grass beneath my feet, so out of place in this jungle hideaway. Benyst lived in the heart of the jungle. A large clearing that was only accessible via the circle we were now standing in or the dangerous path I had first taken oh so long ago.

"You guys wait here," I said to the others.

"I will come with you," Sid said.

"No, you will wait here."

"Benyst and I have been friends a long time. In fact," Sid stared at me hard, "It was I who introduced you."

"If by introduced you mean that you instructed Noiryn to drop me off on his doorstep, then yes, you did that. But he and I have our own history now, and I need to speak to him alone first."

"I disagree."

"Damn it, Sid, am I going to have to pull rank here?"

"No, my lady." He bowed sarcastically at me. I didn't even know it was possible and was honestly a little impressed.

"Wow."

I turned on my heel and walked away. I would have liked to have said something to Archer, but I was too angry at Sid. He seemed to swing pretty sharply from friend to adversary these days. These days? We reconnected forty-eight hours ago. Maybe I was expecting too much, and maybe I hadn't yet let go of the past.

Fortunately, the distance from the circle to Benyst's home was long enough that I could breathe out all the Sid drama and focus on the possible impending Benyst drama. Since he and Noiryn had hooked up, the growths on his face and body had receded to reveal a very handsome man that could grace the cover of any romance novel. The last time I'd seen Benyst I'd made a huge, but impromptu, pass at him. In my defence, he looked ridiculously good, and I was lying on top of him. Long story.

It preoccupied me as I rounded the corner of Benyst's hut and I was caught off guard by the gigantic pool that now lay before it. Pool is the wrong word. It was a beautiful lagoon, so black you couldn't see the bottom and a surface so still the stars reflected in it sparkled. The edges were framed with smooth rocks, some large enough for someone to stretch out on. There was no mistaking it; this was a pool for Noiryn. This was a little sanctuary for her here in the jungle. It warmed my heart.

"I thought I heard something," a smooth, deep voice filled the air.

"Benyst," I said with a smile as I turned to face him.

He looked just as good as he had before, maybe even a little better. His shoulders were broad and heavy with muscle. His arms were thick and defined, and his narrow waist led to muscular legs. His hair was just as long and golden and his face just as handsome, his eyes just as blue.

"You look beautiful," I said.

"You look like shit." Straight to the point, that was Benyst.

"Yes, I do."

"What happened?"

"Is Noiryn here?"

"Nope."

"Can you call her? I'd like to tell you both everything at once."

"All right."

He stepped forward to the edge of the lagoon and stretched his big ropy arms in front of him. I could feel his power coming to life, and soon it was emanating from him in waves. Those waves hit the surface of the water, and it swirled, taking the sparkle of the stars with it and turning into a twisting vortex of darkness and shine. When the vortex had reached a steady rhythm, Benyst dropped his arms and stepped back from the edge of the pool. The water continued to spin as we stood side by side.

"She'll be here soon. She was worried about you."

"She's the best." A heavy pause. "I'm sorry about..."

"Unnecessary," he cut me off. "I reckon we both were at fault there. It's already forgotten."

"Thank you. You didn't tell Noiryn, did you?"

"Of course not! I'm not stupid. Well, not all the time." He winked at me, and it was the pure affection of the man I had met all those weeks ago. No heat, just heart.

"Right." I smiled. It pulled the skin of my face a little too tightly and Benyst, now close enough for a good look, paled slightly.

"Damn," he whispered.

Suddenly the water before us drew in on itself, forming a large spout. The din from the rushing water was intense, and I thought of Archer waiting back at the circle of torches. He was probably doing everything he could to restrain himself from running over here. I glanced over my shoulder, expecting to see him rounding the bend. When I looked back, Noiryn was leaping through the air towards me. I had just enough time to brace myself before her soaking wet arms wrapped around me.

"You're back!" she hugged me tightly, I could feel my newly formed muscles protesting against the pressure.

"Not so tight, Noiryn, I'm still healing."

"Healing?" She stepped back. In her rush to get to me, she hadn't looked at me. She did now, her third eye wide. "Oh no. Oh, Phoenix, what happened to you?"

"Let's all get inside," Benyst said, his hand going to Noiryn's back, guiding her towards the hut. "Phoenix will tell us everything once we've sat down." He turned to me. "And your minions will be fine where they are, no need to worry."

"What about Archer?"

"Oh, he left the second you rounded the corner." Benyst saw the shock on my face. "He must have been called away."

"He better have," I mumbled.

30

Benyst's hut was exactly as I remembered with one recent addition; a beautiful, enormous bed. A bed so big I'd have thought the hut wouldn't have been able to accommodate it.

"Did you expand?" I asked, gesturing at the bed.

"Oh, that's just Traveller magic. Our spaces grow as our needs do."

"They do?" Another Traveller perk I knew nothing about. Sigh.

"Phoenix," Noiryn was practically shoving me into a chair. "What happened to you?"

"Well, it's a bit of a long story, but I'll try to condense things. I went to the City of Caves to stop Greldrom from continuing with the Bounty."

"What?!" Noiryn exclaimed.

"Noiryn, if you interrupt this will take forever," Benyst said as he placed a hand on her scaled thigh.

"I thought Greldrom had set the Bounty, so I challenged him and won. I killed him." I shifted in my seat, Noiryn's third eye burned into me. "And because I killed him, I became the leader of the minions. Archer had come with me to the caves to help, but he'd sort of lost it with all the evil magic there, and took off for the surface. So the minions helped me get out of the Caves. I got to the surface to find Archer fighting with his ex, Mhyr. I stepped into it. And she attacks me. Then it turns out she set the Bounty! She tried some epic magic, powerful stuff, on me and nearly killed me. But, unbeknownst to me, my people get really freaked out when you try to kill them. So freaked out that we have a self-destruct mechanism and Mhyr triggered it. Big time. I burst into flames. I literally exploded and blew everyone out of the area. Then, while I was unconscious, another of my kind," Noiryn made a yelping sound in her throat. "Yep, I couldn't believe it either, an older guy named Royal. Well, he took me home and helped me heal. I was just bone and bits of tendon to start off with, but I've been doing my best to heal the past few days, and now here I am!"

I took a deep breath and let it out.

"That's a lot." Benyst, king of the understatements.

"That's only part of it," Noiryn said. "You glossed over the most significant part."

"Another of my kind?" I asked.

"No," Noiryn shook her head, "You are now the leader of the minions, but I assume the passing of that torch did not go well."

"To put it mildly." I sighed. "There were a couple groups that really did not want me there, and they got violent. I had to put all those against me in the Caves' jail." Noiryn's third eye slowly closed and did not reopen. Not a wonderful sign. "I had them cleaned out first," I added quickly, "And I made sure that someone I could trust was in charge. He has explicit instructions to treat the prisoners well and to contact me the second anything goes wrong." I was practically pleading with Noiryn to approve of my actions because truthfully, I wasn't sure that I did.

"You've done your best," Benyst said gruffly. "I'm surprised you had that in you." He reached across and patted me roughly on the shoulder. "Good work staying alive and smiting your enemies."

"Thanks."

The funny thing about Benyst was that even though all the tumours were gone, and he was this beautiful handsome-romance novel-Greek God looking individual, he still moved like the shy hermit I'd met back at the beginning of this journey. I wondered if he would ever lose that shyness, that undercurrent of unnecessary shame that he had carried for so long.

"What is your next move?" Noiryn asked.

"Well, that's why I'm here. I need your help."

They both just looked at me. No words. No quick 'whatever you need,' they just looked at me.

"Um..." I continued, "I need a team of people I can trust to act as my advisors when I go to the Guard."

"Huh." Benyst made the word deep in his throat.

"You want us to stand beside you and support your actions?" Noiryn asked. I couldn't take the unspoken stuff that was bubbling between us any longer.

"Noiryn, I'm sorry that I have disappointed you. If there had been any other way out of the situation I was in, if I could have avoided going to the City of Caves and killing Greldrom, I would have. But there was no other way. They'd tried to attack me at my family's home. They were hunting me down." I sighed. "Sid thinks someone else was pushing for the encounter, that they were trying to get me to go to the Caves so that Greldrom could kill me."

"Kill you? Why?" she asked.

"Because people think I'm dangerous. And until I figure things out, people will keep trying to kill me." I reached out and took her hand in mine. "I don't like what I did." I could feel tears coming, tears I hadn't allowed myself to shed. "It was a terrible thing to do. But I had to do it. There was no other way out." Tears flowed down my cheeks, Noiryn wiped them away. "I walked out of that hellhole and straight into Mhyr who tried to kill me too. And she almost succeeded. If I hadn't been able to burn up like this, I'd be dead." I looked at Benyst. His cheeks rippled in the firelight. "I need your help. I need the two of you beside me. I can't do this alone."

"We will help you," Noiryn said.

"Of course we will," Benyst agreed.

"Thank you."

Noiryn slid out of her chair and pulled me up into a hug.

"We will come with you now," Noiryn said, turning to Benyst. "We should pack."

"Just give me a minute." He went over to the bed, reached underneath and pulled out a large duffle bag. He swung the bag over his shoulder. "Done. Let's go."

"What about my things?" Noiryn asked.

"Already in here." He patted the bag. "I had a feeling Phoenix would show up eventually and need our help. So I've kept a bag packed for about a week now."

"You are amazing." Noiryn beamed at him, her third eye wide open.

"All right, let's go get the minions and be on our way."

"Are we going straight to the Guard?" Benyst asked.

"No, first we have to go pick up my friend, Royal; the other of my kind that helped me when I first burned. Then I thought we'd head back to my place and have a conversation about what we'll do when we get to the Guard. I'm sure Sid will have some insightful comments for us."

"Sid is here?" Noiryn asked.

"Yeah, he and Spin are waiting in the circle of torches."

"Will the Archer join us?"

"Who knows," Benyst said as he extinguished the various lanterns in the room. "He left almost as soon as Phoenix had stepped out of sight."

"Wow, thanks, Benyst."

"You're welcome," he said seriously as he poured a bucket of water on the fire. Travellers and sarcasm sometimes don't mix.

"Benyst!" Noiryn yelled as acrid white smoke filled the hut. "Let us get outside before you do that!" She took me by the hand and pulled me out the door.

"Noiryn," I said, "Now that we're alone, can I ask you about something?"

"Of course."

"I had a vision a little while ago that I was swimming in the ocean." Her third eye blinked. "Well, I was trying to swim to the bottom of the ocean. I, um, I think I was trying to kill myself. No, I know I was trying to kill myself." She made that same strange throat yelp sound she'd made earlier. "But you were suddenly there, and you stopped me. Thank you for that. What I really want to know is, why did I do it? Had something happened? Had I been depressed? I thought maybe since you were there, you might be able to tell me what had happened."

"All right! Let us depart on our journey!" Benyst stepped joyfully from the hut. "Ladies?" He bowed deeply. "After you."

Noiryn took my hand and pulled me forward. She leant in close and quickly whispered, "We'll talk later."

The minions had heard us coming. Sid was standing tall at the edge of the clearing, waiting for us.

"Sid!" bellowed Benyst. Noiryn dropped my hand as she and Benyst descended on Sid.

"My friends! My friends!" Sid happily scrambled up Benyst's bulk to rest in the crook of his arm. "It is so good to see you! It has been far too long."

I left the three of them chatting and walked over to Spin.

"I'll introduce you once they've finished their love-in." Spin smiled. "What happened with Archer? Why did he leave?"

"He clutched his side, the area where he had drawn that bone, and then said he was getting a message from his people and had to return at once."

"Oh."

"It must have been very important, Phoenix. I have never seen that expression on his face."

"How did he look?"

"Like this." Spin screwed up his little face like he was in pain and then quickly relaxed so his jaw hung open. "And then he did this." He stood up as tall and as straight as he could, his little brow furrowed. "And then he said what he said and left."

"Well, that definitely sounds serious."

"Archer is always serious." Sid's voice sounded behind us. "Most of his kind are."

"Right." I wasn't going to get into it with Sid. "Benyst and Noiryn, this is Spin. He helped me survive when I went into the City of Caves. Spin, this is Benyst and Noiryn."

"Very pleased to meet you," Spin offered his hand to the couple.

"Likewise," Noiryn said with a smile.

"Same," Benyst said.

"All right, we're all here, and we all know each other's names. Time to get Travelling!" I moved to the centre of the clearing and held out my arms. "Grab on and let's get out of here."

Four sets of hands latched onto me. I closed my eyes, and we Travelled.

31

The sun was high in the sky when we landed at Royal's place. The contrast from Benyst's home was so stark that we all immediately clapped our hands over our eyes.

"Damn, it's bright here," Benyst grumbled.

"You didn't tell me we were going to a desert," Noiryn murmured.

"Oh crap, I didn't even think about it." I wiped at my streaming eyes. How could I be so stupid bringing a siren to the desert? She could dry out in minutes. "Will you be okay for a few minutes?"

"A few minutes, yes. But too much longer and I will have a problem."

"We will have a problem," I stressed. "Okay, I'll make this fast. Follow me."

I set out toward Royal's home. The team fell in line behind me with Sid bringing up the rear. We walked over the gentle rise of sand that shielded Royal's home visually from the Travelling spot. Royal was working in his yard, his great wings were paled by the sun. His back was a little stooped, but there was no mistaking him for anything other than one of my kind.

"Oh!" Noiryn breathed, "He looks just like you."

"Just like me is a bit of an overstatement."

"Not really," Benyst chimed in.

As we descended the hill, Royal stopped worked and looked up. A big smile spread across his face as he took in the entire group.

"I thought you'd come," he called up the hill. "I'll get my bag." He turned to go inside.

"Wait," I called back, "Just like that?"

"Just like that."

"How did you know I'd be coming?" I asked as we joined him in the front yard.

"I've got my ways."

Noiryn stepped out from behind me, and Royal did a double take. It was subtle, but it was definitely a double take. She's a beautiful humanoid. It makes sense.

"I'll be right out," he said, then made a beeline for his front door.

"So it's true," Noiryn said as Royal disappeared into his home.

"What is?" I asked.

"There was a rumour, long ago, that a siren loved a man with wings. He clearly has been touched by our kind."

"His wife died," I said.

"Yes, that was how the story went."

"Oh, so Cheryl was a siren?"

"Cheryl?" Noiryn laughed. "No siren would be called, Cheryl."

"He said her name was Cheryl."

"Perhaps he wishes to keep her true self just for him."

"Off we go," Royal called as he locked the door to his house.

"You lock the door?" I asked. "You've got no glass in any of the windows, someone could just walk in. Besides, you're a Traveller, no one can get in without your permission."

"Is that so?" he asked. "Then how did you and your friends just walk right up here?"

"Wait a second, how did we just walk right up here?" I asked, suddenly freaked.

"I don't go in for any of that power shielding nonsense. I lock my door and put the bars up when I leave the place for a while."

"Bars?"

"On the windows." He pointed, and I could now see that yes, bars had appeared on all the windows. "No one thinks I exist. The only people who ever come here already know that I am here, and until now I have sworn them to secrecy. But I guess that's all going to end after we go see the Guard. Are you going to introduce me to everyone?"

"Right, sorry."

Introductions didn't take too long since Royal already knew Sid and Spin. I also wanted to move things along because Noiryn had been standing in the sun for a while and was looking a little dry around the edges. We hastened to the Travelling spot, and everybody put their hands on me. I was trying to think of the perfect joke when Royal leaned in and told me to get a move on.

32

___

We landed well. As well as six humanoids of various sizes can land on a narrow forest path. Yeah, someone elbowed me in the chest a little harder than I would like, not that I enjoy getting elbowed in the chest, but I wasn't going to make a big deal out of it.

"Everybody good?" I asked as I casually rubbed my aching breast.

"We're okay. Looks like you're better," Royal quipped.

"Funny stuff. I took a wild elbow on that landing."

"Sorry about that," Noiryn blushed.

"At least you didn't have this one clinging to your back," Sid jerked a thumb at Spin.

"Hey! My fingers were slipping! I had to hang on to something!"

"Okay! That's enough," I said. "Benyst, you good?"

"Peachy." He pulled a twig out of his hair. Noiryn tried not to giggle.

"Then follow me."

Luckily the path to my home is smooth and clear, and we made great time. I stopped short as we approached the gate. Mastyx was casually leaning against it. He looked exactly the same; tall, lanky, covered in green scales with the head of a snake. A very smug snake.

"Hello," I said.

"Phoenix, you look terrible," he replied, a sly smile stretching out the line of his mouth.

"Thank you."

"I see you have company, so I won't keep you long. May we talk? In private?" He gestured at my gate.

"As if we're going in there." I turned around and started walking. "Come on, Mastyx. We'll do a walk and talk."

"Ssssssigh," he droned but fell in step behind me.

I didn't bother telling the others what to do, and I wasn't going to let the lot of them into my home without me there. At least for the first time. If Archer had been there, then yes, he could have monitored them. 'No, you may not open her refrigerator,' or something like that.

"Shall we sit?" I heard Spin ask the group, and then the sound of the five of them walking into the brush. It looked like Spin's little shelter area would come in handy.

"So," I asked Mastyx as we walked, "What brings you here?"

"Many thingsssssss." Sometimes I think he put a little too much effort into the sibilance thing. "It is strange that the Archer is not with you."

"Why?" I looked at him sharply.

"Oh, don't tell me you've forgotten. You already told me all about the two of you."

"Crap, I forgot."

"Your ssssecret is ssssafe with me. For now."

Mastyx had saved my bacon back when I was dealing

with the Bounty. Mhyr had given me a giant whack on the head and then thrown me out to the Void. Which was where Mastyx had found me, wounded and vulnerable, throwing up on the dark grey ground. He had helped me jump into a stream to get home. It had not been pleasant.

"And just so you know, Travelling by stream sucks. It almost killed me."

"I knew you'd be fine."

"You knew it could kill me?"

"Honey, everything can kill you." He laughed at his own joke. It was a slithering skin creeping sound. "Although, by the looks of you, maybe you can't be killed."

He could only see my face, the rest of me was wrapped up tight. He stepped in front of me and peered into the hood.

"What happened to you?" He smiled. "It lookssssss painful."

"Nope, not at all." Like I'd let him see me sweat.

"Liar." His smile faded a little. "Seriously, what happened Phoenix? I am genuinely concerned. As I have told you, this world is more interesting with you in it."

"Sssssigh," I mimicked, and he laughed. "Fine. Mhyr happened."

"She did this to you!? That bitch!"

"Not directly. She attacked me. It was her that set the Bounty."

"A scorned lover is a dangerous enemy."

"You know about her and Archer?"

"Darling, everyone knows about her and Archer. It was the first time in, oh, a thousand years, that their species had a chance at a True Birth. It was an enormous deal when he ended it."

"He ended it?"

"He didn't tell you?"

"Archer isn't a big sharer when it comes to Mhyr."

"No, I can see why he would avoid the subject."

"So, she attacked me..."

"After you killed Big G."

"You know about that?"

"Darling," he threw up his hands, "I know about everything! But that piece of news was gargantuan and would not have stayed secret for anything in the Universe. Everybody knows."

"Huh. Speaking of things people know, how did you know where I live?"

"I know everything." He looked exasperated. "But continue with your tale, you had killed Big G and were locked in a mortal embrace with the giant chrome muscled Mhyr."

We had reached my Travelling clearing; we stopped walking and turned to each other.

"Right, so I was pretty sure she was going to kill me, and then I just started getting really hot. Super hot. I thought I would melt from the inside out, but instead, I burst into flames and then just kind of exploded."

"Fassssscinating. So you look like this," he reached out and gently touched my cheek with the tip of his finger, "All over?"

"Yep."

"Oh, my darling, Phoenix, I am so sorry."

"Don't be. It used to be much worse. Seriously worse. Like skeletal worse."

"Ew."

"Exactly. I'm doing much better now and getting stronger every day. So, let's get right to it, the reason why you are here."

"Go on," he smiled.

"It's obvious to anyone with half as many informants as you, you're here to talk about me joining the Guard."

"Yes. I am." He just stared at me.

"So... Make with the talk."

"My dear, at times you have a terrible sense of language."

"And at times I'm a bloody poet. You've been good to me, Mastyx, but you haven't really been nice to me. So let's get to the meat of the conversation."

"Nice?" He rolled the word around his mouth like he had never heard it before. Maybe he hadn't.

"It's a way some humans like to treat each other, and a way most humans like being treated."

"I know what nice is, bird." He was getting pissed. "To my mind, I have been nice to you. Nicer to you than I have been to many others."

"You left me at Cosima's place to die!"

"No, not die. I had no doubt in your ability to beat her."

"But you left me on the beach with no way to get out of there."

"And yet, get out of there you did."

I took a deep breath and counted to a thousand, okay, three.

"Moving on, is there something specific you'd like to discuss regarding my joining the Guard?"

"Yes. Don't do it."

"Okay."

"I'm serious."

"Yes, I can see that, but Mastyx, what the hell else am I going to do? I have to join. I killed Big G, which made me the leader of the minions."

"You don't have to take the chair. I'm sure many Minions would happily battle it out for a chance at the position."

"I'm not comfortable with that."

"Comfortable with what?"

"With leaving the minions to their violent ways. I was in the City of Caves, I saw firsthand just how disgusting it was. Big G treated them like garbage, and they treated each other even worse." I lowered my voice. "They chained Sid to a wall. And Spin…" I took a breath, "Terrible things happened to them under Greldrom's rule."

"Greldrom was not the cause of their violence, Phoenix. He only allowed it to continue. There have been other leaders before him, and each was just as terrible as Big G. His death will not change them." He paused. "Nor will you."

"But not all of them want the violence! Some of them, a good many, were happy I was there! They were relieved that Greldrom was gone. What about them?"

"Then perhaps you should build a village for them on your doorstep, and they can all live in harmony with you here." I shot him a look. "Again, I am serious. You cannot change them all, and if some are finished with their lives of violence and pain, perhaps the most humane thing would be for them to leave the Caves all together?"

"Can I do that? Can I split up a species?"

"Well, that I do not know. It has never been done. But it would certainly be interesting." He smiled.

"And you love interesting."

"You know it, babe."

"Either way, keep them together or break them apart, I have to take a seat on the Guard to make that happen, yes?"

"Well, yes."

"Any tips on making that go smoothly?"

"The Archer has not discussed this with you?"

"Oh, your fishing trips are so subtle."

"Guilty," his tongue flicked out. "But based on your

response, that is a no. He has not given you his council. So I shall give you mine." He paced the clearing. "It will not be easy. Cosima will most definitely throw an epic fit."

"Well, I knew that."

"I am unsure of how the others will respond. I cannot recall an occasion where a member of another species has taken the chair on their behalf. I would keep your thoughts of splitting the minions to yourself."

"Um, that's your idea."

"Yes, and you should think about it. It's an excellent one." He continued, "I would keep that thought to yourself and focus on taking the chair to represent them all. I'm not sure what the Guard will decide, but there will most definitely be a challenge or trial of some sort."

"Why? I already killed Big G."

"Because, they, we," he purred, "are powerful and strong and can do whatever we want." He stroked his chest. "So I would bring as many allies with you as you can, to show that you are no longer alone in the Void. That may help."

"May?"

"This isn't an exact science, my dear. You seem to have a knack for creating problems with which we have never dealt." He looked me up and down. "So interesting. Do you think we will ever...?" He wiggled the ridge of flesh above his eyes at me.

"Nope."

"Never?"

"Never."

"Is it the scales?" He played with his chest some more.

"Nope, it's just a general personality conflict."

"I thought I was being nice." He dropped his arms. "Can we at least be friends?" More wiggling.

"I'll think about it."

"Well, that I will take." He bowed low. "Goodbye, Phoenix. I will see you again soon."

"Thanks, Mastyx."

Then he was gone.

33

———

I walked back with Mastyx's advice spinning through my brain. Upon reflection, it wasn't much: bring a team and be prepared for a challenge. The story of my life. It would be nice if Archer could be part of that team, but that wasn't possible right now.

I needed to get myself on the Guard. Once I established there, we could reveal our relationship, and then I could start changing the rules. Like not outlawing healing across the species, and maybe even allowing the healing of humans and animals when we Travelled.

I flashed back to one of my first wing visions: I was in a dungeon watching women being interrogated, aka tortured, for being something a bunch of dumb men couldn't under-stand. They had burned her at the stake. I had wanted so badly to help, to take her pain away, and I couldn't. My powers couldn't cross over to her. It broke my heart. But to help them, to save them like I wanted to, would have changed history and caused ripples throughout time; the consequences of which could not be foreseen. Which was a real bitch.

When I got back to my gate, I found my friends sitting in a comfortable circle around a fire that Spin was tending to. He looked up from his work and saw me.

"You're back!" Spin smiled.

"I'm back."

"How did it go?" Benyst asked. Noiryn was leaning on his shoulder. She looked, for lack of a better term, dry.

"Tell you inside. Noiryn, are you okay?"

"Just a little dry," she replied. Huh, I was right.

"Okay, let's get you inside. I have a wicked bathtub."

"Oh," she said as Benyst scooped her up into his arms. "The tub," she continued, "what did it do?"

"Do?"

"You said it was wicked." It took me a second.

"Sorry, it's a human expression, it means great."

"That makes little sense," Benyst grumbled.

"No, I guess it doesn't."

Our rag-tag group had made it to the gate. Spin bringing up the rear after putting out the cooking fire. I asked Spin where he'd found the water.

"Oh, I just peed on it," he replied.

"Efficient," Royal quipped.

My five friends gathered around me in front of the gate. I looked at Sid.

"Is there something formal I have to do to let you in?"

"No."

"Okay," I stepped aside and gestured to the gate. "Come on in."

Nobody moved.

"Welcome my friends!" I said as formally as I could muster.

Again, nobody moved.

"Are you guys coming in or what?"

"You have to go through first," Sid answered.

"That would have been helpful info, you know when I'd asked for it."

"I do not consider walking through a gate a 'formal' activity," he replied.

I shrugged and walked through the gate. I think I heard Royal mutter 'this is going to be great' as he trailed behind me.

34

─────

My home was as beautiful and majestic as always. The sturdy stone walls rose into the sky, and the sun glinted off the roof of the greenhouse, its colossal glass bulk filled with trees. The wide stone steps welcomed me forward, and I crossed the lawn with quick steps, eager to lay my hand on the warm wood of the epic front door. My foot hit the first tread of the steps when a loud splashing sound filled the air.

"What was that?" I spun around. The group stretched behind me in a haphazard line, Benyst's arms were now empty. "Where's Noiryn?"

"You didn't tell me you had a pond!" she called.

"I guess I just thought you'd prefer the bath." Although the pond was beautiful, it had a significant amount of green slime around the edges.

"This is better!" Noiryn disappeared under the water.

I got the boys inside. They made sounds of appreciation and wonder as they explored the lower level, with Spin exclaiming that everything was 'beautiful!' and 'so clean!' As they looked around, I noticed Sid standing outside the door of the greenhouse. He was just staring at the door.

"What's up, Sid?"

"There is a substantial power beyond this door."

"It's a special place to me."

"That is clear." He turned to me, his eyes were gleaming. "I would suggest you lock this door."

"Why?" I said cautiously.

"Because this power is not something you should share."

"But is it something someone would take?"

"Yes." He looked back at the door. "I'm not sure I can restrain myself."

"What?"

"You must lock this door."

"I don't think I have a key."

"Lock it with your power!" his voice was a harsh whisper. "Really, Phoenix, you must embrace what you are!"

"Who. Who I am."

"Semantics. Lock this door."

I looked at Sid. His breathing had become ragged, and his back heaved with it. As I watched, he reached out and made to place his hand on the door, but at the last moment stopped.

"Sid, what's going on?"

"I cannot deny what I am," he replied. "I am a minion, and we are creatures that take. Please lock the door."

"Okay, I will."

"Thank you." He quickly shuffled out of the room.

"That was interesting," Royal's quiet voice sounded behind me.

"How much of that did you hear?"

"All of it." He stepped up beside me. "He may want to be

your friend, but can't handle what a friendship with you entails."

"What do you mean?"

"You're a powerful person, Phoenix. And loyal. You love deeply, quickly and fiercely."

"I guess so." He smiled.

"Some Travellers can't handle that, they don't know what it means, or how they should act. You'd known me two minutes, and you trusted me completely. I could have been a complete psycho, but you trusted me."

"You didn't give me a reason not to."

"Not yet." He smiled.

"Not yet." I smiled back.

"And God help me if I do."

"God? I didn't know Travellers had God."

"Just a turn of phrase I picked up watching humans."

"Right."

"I'll keep an eye on Sid and make some dinner."

"Thank you."

"You're welcome. Now lock that door." I opened my mouth to ask how. "Just walk up to it, call your power, and picture the door sealed."

"Thanks."

He nodded and walked away.

I looked at the door. It looked back at me. Okay, it didn't. But I wouldn't rule anything out anymore. I put my palms on the door and spread my fingers wide. The wood felt warm and solid under my hands. I ran my hands all over it, feeling every inch. As I caressed the wood, I called to it. I told it what I intended to do, what I need from it, how much I valued its contribution to my safety and peace of mind. I sweet-talked the hell out of that door and meant every word. I'd have to be a complete idiot to miss that intention was an enormous part of making power work. I had to believe deep in the core of my soul, or the magical locking of this door would never happen. I had to believe that the door was in this with me. Together we would lock it. Together we would keep my greenhouse safe.

"Okay, time to make some magic," I whispered to the door.

In my mind's eye, I reached down into the centre of my body, below my heart: the place where all my vital systems connected, the place where my body flowed from one meridian to the other. I reached into that place, and I called forth my power. After our recent journey through the caves, my energy was simmering, just waiting for another chance to let loose.

My power came quickly in a bright blue wave that flowed through my body, washing clean any tension my muscles held. I took a deep breath, my ribs moving smoothly under the grey of my jumpsuit. My wings stretched at my back, bucking slightly at their fabric casings. The blue wave moved through my brain, calming my mind and focusing my thoughts. I closed my eyes and willed my power into my hands, then fingers, then out into the wood.

The blue changed to green as it contacted the old oak and flowed through the channels that had once been filled with water and sap. The wood still held its own power like all great wood does, and through my eyelids, I could see the door glow green as our powers mingled. The wood allowed me entry; it welcomed me, and soon we were joined. The door was alive and linked to me. It would only open to my call. It would only yield to me and I to it. I would not allow low energy to cross its threshold, and it would not allow those without permission to pass through.

We sealed our pact there in the quiet entryway and then

the power receded, pulled back to my belly as the wood returned to its slumber.

I stepped back from the door and took a deep breath. In one day I had become bonded to a minion and a door. Things in my life were getting stranger at an exponential rate, and yet, I felt great. I felt centred. I felt more myself than I ever had. More myself than I had ever felt when I was a human. And maybe that was it, maybe I had to finally accept that I never had been human. I was out of place in that world, so easily dismissed as the black sheep, the odd one out, the weird one, when I just was a saltwater fish in a freshwater pond.

Now that I had found my home, my power, myself, I felt better than ever.

I heard laughter coming from the kitchen and drifted toward it, every step I took landing solidly on the stone floor of my home.

35

Noiryn was standing in the centre of the kitchen looking radiant, wrapped in a big fluffy towel I recognized from my bathroom upstairs. Her third eye was open, and it stayed trained on Benyst, who was laughing around a mouthful of Royal's cooking. Royal had his back to me as he stood over the stove, his shoulders shaking with mirth. Spin was sitting on the large island in the middle of the room, picking at a plate of food and laughing. Even Sid chuckled from his chair at the kitchen table.

"What's so funny?" I asked.

"Noiryn was just telling us about some humans," Spin answered.

"Humans? Do tell," I sat down at the island and Royal had a plate of food in front of me before I could ask.

"Oh, I was just telling them about the time I saw a group of humans line up to jump one at a time from a board into the water."

Evidently, diving boards make no sense to Travellers.

"Yes, humans are into that kind of thing."

"Why aren't you laughing like we did?" Spin asked.

"Because Phoenix was a human," Sid said. The room quieted.

"You were?" Spin's eyes widened.

"Sorry, Spin, I thought everybody knew. I lived as a human for about thirty years before these guys," I pointed at Sid, Noiryn and Benyst, "helped me regain my wings."

"And now you're a Traveller?"

"Well, now I think I'm something in between."

"Cool!" He tucked back into his food, no more answers necessary.

"You look much better," I said to Noiryn.

"Your pond is fantastic. A little green though, I had to take a quick shower after I'd had my fill. I hope you don't mind."

"Not at all." I finally took a bite of the pasta Royal had made. "This is amazing!"

"Thank you," he said as he puttered around the kitchen.

"Where did you get the gargoyles statues?" Noiryn asked. My fork stopped halfway to my mouth. "It's so interesting how you have them sitting in the fireplace like that."

"Um... I'll be right back."

I pushed back from the island and was out of the room before they could ask me any more questions.

As I climbed the stairs, I thought about the gargoyles. I loved the little guys; they had helped me so much. It was time that they became a part of every aspect of my life. It was time to free the gargoyles from whatever magic held them and introduce my little friends to my friends of various sizes.

I locked the bedroom door behind me and made a beeline for the bathroom. I locked that door behind me too and hurried over to the fireplace. Grog and Brog were as I'd left them; on the edges of the grate just inside the hearth, nestled amongst the glowing embers.

"Guys? Can you wake up, please?"

Nothing.

"Guys?"

Grog cracked open a single eye and whispered.

"Is she gone?"

"Who?"

"The siren."

"She's downstairs with the others."

"Others?" Brog yelped.

"Guys, it's okay. I've locked both doors; no one can get in here."

"But they could hear us," Grog whispered.

"That's why I'm here." Both gargoyles now had a single eye open and were staring at me, their bodies remained like statues. "I'd like to introduce you to them."

"What!" Brog sat up straight.

"Brog!" Grog sat up straight. "We're not supposed to move!"

"Sorry!" Brog froze, but he was sitting upright, and his eyes were as wide as saucers. It wasn't much of a cover.

"It's okay, guys. I'd like you to talk to my friends, to come to life around them."

"Why?" Grog looked suspicious.

"Because you are super important to me, you are my friends, my family."

The gargoyles looked at each other; it was Brog that spoke.

"No one's ever said that before." A little pebble fell from the corner of his eye. It bounced on the hearth, and I caught it.

"Will you please reveal yourselves to my friends?"

"Grog?" Brog looked at his brother.

"Once we do this it cannot be undone, they will always know we are alive."

"I think it might be nice to have friends," Brog shuffled forward and put his arms around Grog. "We can trust Phoenix, she's been very good to us, she's kept us safe."

"She has," Grog took a deep breath, his little stone chest rising and falling, Brog moving with it.

"So, you'll do it?" I asked.

"Yes. We will," Grog said.

"Okay, what do I have to do?"

"Do?" Brog asked.

"Yeah, to break the spell and stuff."

"My lady," Grog said, "there is no spell."

"Oh, so you guys can just come to life whenever you want?"

"Pretty much," Brog beamed.

"So why didn't you come to life when I carried you back here?"

The gargoyles looked at each other, Grog answered for them.

"You looked nice, but we had to be sure."

"Oh, okay, makes sense. I thought it was like some big magical thing." I stood up. "Well, would you guys like to come downstairs?"

"Very much!" Brog practically bounced to the bathroom door.

36

Brog ran like a toddler in a rolling series of mini falls while trying to keep his big head upright. He and Grog both have giant heads for the size of their bodies, which can be problematic. Brog had the added issue of the chunk of stone missing from the top of his skull. Grog was agile and focused. He stayed right on Brog and made sure he didn't hit any walls or lag too far behind, but he did it in a way that felt natural, which I guess it was.

When we got to the top of the stairs, I paused.

"You guys okay going down the stairs?"

"Yes," Grog answered, "we have done it many times."

"It's my favourite," Brog smiled and then with a level of agility I hadn't expected, he climbed up the stair post and then onto the bannister.

"You slide down?"

"It's great!" he smiled and slid down the bannister.

"Wait for me," Grog slid down after Brog.

"And me." I trotted quickly down after them.

When we got to the foyer, I could hear the others talking in the kitchen.

"Okay, wait outside the kitchen until I get you."

"Yes, my lady," Grog's face was very serious.

"It will be okay, Grog," I smiled. He nodded.

I hovered in the kitchen doorway and waited until the conversation in the room had died down.

"Hi guys," I said. They all looked at me.

"Hello," said Benyst.

"What is it?" Noiryn asked.

"Well, I have some friends I'd like you to meet."

"They are here, in the house?" Sid asked, his spine straightening.

"Yes, they live here with me. We are very close, and I'd like them to be a part of what we're doing here. I'd like you all to meet them."

"Then let's go," Spin moved to get down from the island.

"That's okay, wait here."

I walked out to the hallway to find the gargoyles sitting huddled together just outside the spill of light from the kitchen. I knelt down in front of them.

"You guys ready to do this?"

"Yep!" Brog said, and then without warning, he climbed onto my lap and up into my arms. I had a moment to brace myself against his weight when Grog scrambled up after him.

"Um, so I'm carrying you in?"

"Yes, please," Grog whispered. He shivered ever so slightly. I hadn't realised just how scared he was.

"Grog, Brog, it will be okay. These are good people. But if you don't like them or need to go back to being statues when they're around, that's okay too. You can even just hide out in my rooms if that's what you need."

"Thank you," Grog's voice was a little stronger, "let us go meet your friends. But first," he pulled away from me, "I think I shall walk in." He climbed out of my arms. "Just don't go too far."

"Cool," I smiled and then stood with Brog in my arms.

I walked into the kitchen, Grog right on my heels.

"Guys, this is Brog and Grog."

The others were quiet as I put Brog down on the island. Grog tugged on my pant leg, and I lifted him up to sit beside Brog. I leant against the counter so the gargoyles could lean against me.

"Hello, Brog. Hello, Grog," Noiryn said. Her third eye drifted over them. "It's a pleasure to meet you. I'm Noiryn."

"It is nice to meet you, Noiryn," Grog said. His voice was back to its robust gravel sound.

"I'm Benyst. Pleased to meet you."

"And you," Brog smiled.

Spin scooted forward and reached out his hand.

"I am Spin." The gargoyles didn't move.

"He wants to shake your hand, like this." I reached out and shook Spin's hand.

"Cool!" Brog reached out and vigorously shook Spin's hand.

"Nice shake!" Spin smiled and turned to Grog, who shook his hand in a much more controlled fashion.

"You guys hungry?" Royal put a plate of rocks in front of the gargoyles. "I'm Royal." He winked and went back to the stove.

"Thank you!" Brog tucked into the rocks, Grog picked one up and sniffed it.

"You guys eat rocks?" I asked.

"Yes," Grog said.

"How did you know they eat rocks?" I asked Royal.

"I've met their kind before."

"You have?" Grog asked quickly, his eyes bright.

"Oh yeah, a long time ago, I met a couple of you in an old castle. Good guys."

"Do you remember their names?" Grog asked.

"Hmm, let's see, Quar and Quart, I think."

"We know them!" Brog exclaimed. A little pebble fell out of his mouth and bounced along the island.

"They are distant cousins," Grog explained.

It was at this point that I realised Sid hadn't introduced himself. I looked over to where he had been sitting, but the chair was empty.

"Where's Sid?"

"He's right here," Noiryn turned and then stopped short. "He was here."

"He slipped out after you left the room," Benyst said.

"What? Why?"

"I do not know. He slipped to the floor and hugged the wall as he left. I assumed he did not want to be seen." Benyst had picked up the pebble that had fallen from Brog's mouth and was examining it. He gave it a sniff and then popped it in his mouth. He saw me watching him and shrugged. "They seem to like them."

"I'm going to go look for Sid. You guys okay here?" I asked the gargoyles. They were deep in conversation with Spin.

"Oh yes, he's fun," Brog said.

"Don't be long," Grog said in a quiet voice.

"I won't be," I patted his back. It was cold and hard. "Royal? Can you come with me, please?" He nodded, wiped his hands on a towel and walked out to the hallway. I turned to Noiryn. "Why don't you guys move through to the living room? Brog and Grog make a brilliant fire."

"We do," Grog said. "Can you lift us down, please?"

"I can do it," Noiryn and moved towards them. "If that's okay."

Grog looked at her shrewdly and then nodded. There was a lot of nodding going on; we would need a chiropractor on site soon. I left them to it and went out to the hall to find Royal. He had lit the lanterns, and the hall now glowed with a warm yellow light. The light played with the colours in his wings, making him look like a weathered angel, touched with light yet worn by time.

"So, where do you think he went?" I asked him.

"It doesn't really matter where he went. The important question is why did he go."

"Huh, I hadn't thought of that. Why do you think he left?"

"Something is going on here that he doesn't like, or there's something here that he likes very much."

"The greenhouse. But I locked the door. He can't get in there."

"Okay, then something is going on here that he doesn't like."

"Like what?"

"Well, it seems to me that he was used to having you all to himself. And now you've got a lot of friends. And he was also used to you being very weak and dependent on him, and the people he approved of, who were coincidentally also weak when he approved of them. But now you're stronger, in control, and the people he chose to help you have grown stronger and more whole in his absence. He's not in control anymore."

"Wow. I didn't think he could be that petty."

"It's just a theory. Like his theory that someone set you up in the Caves."

"How did you know about that?" I asked sharply.

"Honey, he told you in my house. I hear everything in my house."

"So what do you think?"

"I think he's right."

"You do?"

"Yep, that place is one of the oldest strongholds in Traveller history. It's beyond powerful. And you just waltzed in there..."

"Like the wind."

"Exactly."

"So what do I do about Sid?"

"First, we find him. Second, we talk to him."

"We?"

"I'm standing here, aren't I?"

"Yep."

37

We did a quick search of the upper floor, Royal checking under the beds and me handling the closets. I didn't think Sid would hide under a bed or in a closet, but we needed to be sure. It was also a good way to refresh myself with the layout of the house. I had spent little time here, and it felt excellent to see that not only did I have seven bedrooms, each one had an ensuite bathroom. Swanky. There was only one downside.

"How am I going to clean all of this?" I muttered to no one in particular.

"You don't," Royal answered.

"Won't it get gross?"

"Nope, every once in a while you just toss some power over everything, and it cleans itself."

"Oh, that's convenient."

"Sure is. Let's check downstairs."

We didn't have any luck down there either. We could hear the group in the living room. They were laughing and talking, Grog's gravelly voice rising and falling as he told a story.

We doubled back to the kitchen, but no Sid. We checked the weapons room; I was sure we would find him there. But nothing. We checked the door to the greenhouse. It was still locked up tight.

Sid wasn't in the house.

"Time to check the yard." Royal was out the door before I could agree.

It was dark out, near midnight by the deepness of the night sky and the brightness of the stars.

"No moon," I said.

"I think you've had enough moon for a while," Royal smiled. In the dark, his teeth were a ghostly white.

"We should have brought a flashlight," I said.

"You've got to get in the game, girl," Royal raised his hand, and a ball of bright white light appeared. It illuminated the surrounding area.

"That is so cool."

"So do it," he quipped.

"How?"

Royal doused his light ball and put his hands on his hips.

"Just, do it."

I huffed out a sigh and held my hand in front of my face. I looked at it and thought 'light ball.' I felt a slight sizzling sensation in my palm, and a ball of bright green light appeared in my hand.

"Cool!"

"Yep, you just gotta work on the colour." The green light made Royal look like he was going to puke. I'm sure I didn't look much better.

"Right." I stared hard at the ball of light and thought 'white.' The green flickered and then settled into a bright white light.

"Good. Now let's look for Sid."

We walked the grounds around the house and even grabbed a big stick and dragged it through the pond, but no Sid.

"Maybe he left?" I dropped the ball of light into my left hand and shook out the right. It was getting hot.

"Let's go see."

Royal took off across the lawn, his long strides making quick work of the distance to the gate. He crossed through without a pause, and I joined him on the other side.

"There he is," Royal pointed.

And there he was. Sid. He was sitting on a log in the little shelter area Spin had created. He sat before a fire, unmoving, staring into the flames.

"I'd better go talk to him."

"I'll stay right here," Royal said, not taking his eyes off of Sid.

"Thank you."

I extinguished my ball of light and stepped off the path and into the brush. There was no way to hide my approach. The brush rustled with my every move, and the twigs under my feet popped at regular intervals. Sid had to know I was approaching, and yet he didn't move. I entered the campsite and took a seat on a log opposite him. I looked across the fire at his compact frame. He looked sad and angry. Sangry. It's like 'hangry,' but much harder to rectify.

"Sid?" He blinked but didn't answer me. "Sid? Are you okay?"

And then we sat there. I gave him time to answer. Maybe 'are you okay?' was a harder question for him than I realised. I sat in silence and waited. Finally, he spoke.

"I don't think so." His voice was dry. It was creepy to hear him speak without the usual pile of phlegm.

"What's wrong?"

"I don't feel right. I feel angry."

"What are you angry about?"

"You misunderstand me. I am not angry about something, I am anger. My heart is anger. My heart wants anger."

"Oh." This was getting scary, I was glad Royal was nearby. I could just make out his wings framed by the gate.

"My heart wants violence." Sid looked at me. His eyes were bloodshot and intense. It chilled me, and I recoiled at the strength of his gaze.

"You see it. I know you do. I tried to fight it, but since our return to the Caves, the feeling has grown."

"The Caves? Do you think a spell there infected you?"

He laughed, it was mirthless.

"Oh, I wish that were true. No, I have not been infected. I have been revealed."

"What do you mean, Sid? You're scaring me."

"I belong with my kind."

"The minions? But we're liberating them."

"You are so foolish," his voice sounded harsh, like rough stone dragged across the pavement. "You will only be able to rule the weak, the ones at the bottom of the pile, the carrion."

"Sid, what are you saying?"

"You do not have the power."

"Okay, we've been over this, Sid. You need to stop treating me like a helpless..." Sid cut me off.

"You are weak, you are nothing, you are not strong enough and never will be. I will lay claim to the City, and I will lay claim to the Minion Throne. And if you get in my way, I will stop you."

Venom dripped from his every word. It shocked me, and I stammered my response.

"What? Sid? You can't be serious."

He stood.

"I will own my people."

He was serious. Deadly serious. Something in me clicked. Something in me became deeply calm, and I stood, my wings spread. Power rolled in my belly, a deep red power that steadied my legs and steeled my heart. I looked Sid dead in the eyes, the flames flashing between us.

"Bring it, bitch."

He hissed a horrible guttural sound, then ran off into the darkness.

38

———————

"Fuck!" I bellowed into the night.

I could hear Royal running through the brush, the trees made flying impossible.

"Phoenix! Are you all right?" he panted, concern painted all over his face.

"No. I am not fucking all right." I was breathing hard. I had to get a grip on myself.

"What happened?" Royal asked.

"We need to get inside the gate," I looked around; it was pitch black beyond the firelight. Sid could be anywhere. "We need to get to the others, now."

"Okay. Breathe a little slower for me, honey," I shot him a look. "Please."

I forced a breath deep into my lungs and then let it out as slowly as I could with my heart going ape-shit in my chest. It took a few goes before I was calm enough to speak again.

"We need to put out the fire," I said.

"Good, real good," Royal nodded at my now calm

manner. "I've got it covered." With a simple movement of his hand, he doused the fire, the ashes cold and black.

"How did you do that?"

"I'll show you later," he scanned the trees. "Let's move."

We crossed the brush and made it through the gates without incident.

"How do I revoke Sid's invitation?"

"Huh, I thought things had gone bad. Do it like you did with the door, but as quick as you can."

My breathing may have calmed down, but I was still thrumming with power. I held my arm out to the gate and thought of Sid's ugly hissing face and a gigantic bolt of bright red power shot from my hand. It hit the gate with a loud bang and a shower of red sparks that lit up the sky.

"Or you could go big," sarcasm dripped from Royal's words.

"We're lucky I didn't blow the thing up," I quipped.

The door to the house burst open, Benyst charged across the lawn towards us. Noiryn was hot on his heels. In the darkness, her third eye was a bright white beacon.

"What's going on?" Benyst bellowed.

"Are you guys okay?" Noiryn asked.

I looked past them to see Spin and the gargoyles venturing out onto the porch with scared looks on their faces.

"Get back inside," I called.

"Why?" Noiryn asked.

"I'll explain inside," I strode up the lawn, Royal beside me.

Noiryn turned, picking Brog up on her way through the door. Benyst hadn't moved.

"Now, Benyst."

It must have been a combination of the look on my face

and the power in my veins because Benyst turned and walked back inside without a word.

"Remember how you did that, honey," Royal whispered to me.

I closed the door behind me. I wanted to feel the lock turn under my hand and give it an extra seal of power. Everyone was standing behind me, waiting for me to tell them what was going on. I said nothing.

I walked down the main hall and into my dining room, a sizeable space with a coffered ceiling done in dark wood. The walls were painted a deep royal blue. Down the centre of the room was a large table the same wood of the ceiling. It could easily seat twelve. I walked to the head of the table and sat down. The others milled around in the doorway.

"Please, sit down."

Royal was the first to make a move. He walked with an easy confidence down the room and took the seat on my right. My newly minted right-hand man. Noiryn followed him; she put Brog down on the table and then sat on my left. Benyst sat beside her. Grog and Spin climbed onto the table, so the two gargoyles and Spin sat facing me. We were a tight circle in the cavernous room.

"Okay, guys," I started, "I'm sorry if I scared you out there, but something big just went down."

"Where's Sid?" Spin looked frightened.

"He left," I sighed. "I'm sorry, Spin. He won't be coming back. He said that he felt a great anger inside himself, that he had felt it growing since he was in the Caves. He said that he was no longer on my side. He," the words caught in my throat, "he said that he wanted to rule the minions, to take the throne, to own them. And he said if I got in his way, he would take me down."

Noiryn gasped. Spin launched into a coughing fit. Benyst

got up from the table, so fast his chair fell over, and Grog put his arms around Brog.

"Why would he say such things?" Noiryn asked no one in particular.

"Places of power can do strange things to some minds," Royal's reassuring baritone rolled through the room. "He struck me as a stronger fella, but you never can tell."

"What are we going to do?" Benyst righted his chair and sat back down.

"Thank you for saying 'we.'"

"Of course," Noiryn spoke, "we're not going anywhere."

"Agreed," Spin's voice was quiet but clear. "You can't abandon the minions now, Phoenix. You just can't."

"I'm not going to, Spin. I saw what things were like in the Caves. I'm taking that seat on the Guard. Sid can blow me," Noiryn gasped, Royal chuckled. "Not everybody there wanted it that way, but enough of them liked the violence and debauchery that Sid will be able to put up a hell of a fight."

"You should bring them here!" Spin said.

"What?"

"The ones that will follow you, I mean. Bring them here, and we can set up camp outside the gates. Then you can keep us safe."

"That's exactly what Mastyx said."

"He's a smart guy," Royal said.

"Seriously?" I asked.

"Yep, he's been on the Guard a long time with no challenges from his people, and no wars with any other group. He's an excellent strategist."

"It is a sound idea, Phoenix," Benyst said. "They could live comfortably in the forest outside the gates."

I looked at Noiryn.

"What do you think?"

"It makes the most sense. It's not ideal, but you can handle it," she smiled, but it looked forced.

"But what happens when Sid comes for me?" I asked the group.

"You don't have the take the seat on the Guard," Benyst said. "If you give it to Sid, there will be no reason for war."

"I repeat: Sid can blow me. If Sid is their ruler, he may try to order the defectors back, and who knows what horrible things he'd do to them."

We sat in silence as we each pondered the fresh hell Sid would rain down on the most vulnerable of the minions.

"So," Royal's voice broke the silence, and we all jumped a little, "It's settled. You will go claim your seat on the Guard as leader of the minions, and we're going to the get the minions who want to leave and bring them over here."

"Right," I stood up, "Let's go."

"Right now?" Noiryn asked.

"Yes, now," I replied. "We don't know when Sid will move on his plan, and I don't want Rogmesh and the others having to fight him on their own."

"We will need to move sizeable groups of them quickly," Benyst said. "Phoenix, you cannot expect to move each one yourself."

"Phoenix and I can introduce you all, and then everyone can help bring my people over," Spin said. "I can coordinate everyone here, and Rogmesh can help me."

"That's a brilliant idea," I said. "We'll all go to the Caves first and get started with the move, and while you guys handle that, Royal and I will go to the Guard. Agreed?" Everyone nodded. "Great. Go gather what you need, and we'll meet out on the lawn."

39

Everyone sprang into action. Benyst took Noiryn by the hand, and they moved swiftly from the room, Royal muttered something about supplies and slipped out after them, Spin hot on his heels.

"I need to change," I said to myself. My suit had gotten ruined down in the Caves, I really should have changed hours ago.

"Do you require help?" Grog asked.

"Good thinking, yes, I do need your help. Come on."

I scooped the two gargoyles off the table and made quick work of the stairs. The gargoyles hung on tight all the way up to my room. I sat down on the bed and Brog sliced me free of the old suit with his sharp nails, while Grog started rummaging through the closets.

I looked in the mirror as Brog exposed my flesh to the glass. I still looked shocking, but I was getting used to it. Sort of. I could handle my face. It looked okay. It was my torso that gave me pause. With a quick tug, Brog had freed my wings, and the top of my suit fell down, exposing my deflated breasts. I had no belly button, just a smooth expanse of muscle covered with a thin layer of epidermis. I could still see the outline of each of my ribs, shifting with every breath.

Another tug and my anaemic chicken wing like arms were visible. Brog nudged me to my feet, and soon I could see my legs, so chorded with muscle that you could see each one twitch as I moved. I needed some body fat, ASAP. I couldn't even look at my ass. With only muscle over the bone, it was misshapen and flat.

"Phoenix? We are ready for you," Grog said, breaking me from my negative thought spiral.

"Right," I pulled my eyes from the mirror and gasped.

Grog had found another suit. A beautiful suit. I knelt beside him, taking the fabric in my hand. It was dark black velvet, soft as a kitten, you know I like kitten softness, and lined with smooth cotton that I just knew would lay beautifully against my thin skin. I held the sleeve to my face and rubbed the lining against it.

"It's so soft," I whispered.

"Check out the wings!" Brog held up one of the wing flaps. They were covered with black gemstones and sparkled brightly, even in the soft light of the room.

"This is amazing. Where did you find it?"

"It was in the final closet, near the end," Grog said. "There are also matching boots."

He held them up. They were also black velvet and looked like they went to mid-thigh. A row of gems ran up the back of the boots like a seam. They had subtle rugged soles, perfect for running through the Void.

"And gloves too!" Brog held up short black velvet gloves. A small gemstone sat at the tip of each finger, like sparkly nail polish.

"They're amazing. It's all amazing! Let's get me in it!"

The boys made quick work of getting me into the fantastic suit. It looked even better on. The black velvet added dimension to the parts of me that were still super boney and shape where I had none. Gotta love pre-human Phoenix. She knew how to dress.

Grog had also found a matching holder for my sword, though without my hair the hilt was visible. The suit's hood was more like a cowl, and around the edge was another spray of black gemstones. When I pulled it up, it framed my face and made me look like a glamorous Grim Reaper.

"Come sit on the bed so we can get the boots on," Brog said.

When Brog had a particular task, he was quite the focused little gargoyle. His tiny stony fingers made quick work of the boot's zipper. When all the pieces were in place, the three of us stood in front of the mirror and admired our work.

"You look amazing," Brog whispered.

"I really do, don't I?" I said.

"Beautiful and deadly," Grog added.

That summed it up perfectly. The glittering gems on my wings were almost as beautiful as my feathers, almost. I turned in front of the mirror, and the light danced across the various gems on my body. I felt beautiful and tough for the first time in weeks.

"Thank you guys, I couldn't have gotten in this without you."

"You're welcome," Grog said.

"Shall we show the others?" Brog asked.

"Hell yeah!" I said.

Noiryn freaked out when she saw the suit. She squealed and made me do three twirls so she could take it all in, but pointedly ignored the blade at my back. Royal whistled and

Spin asked to touch one of the gems. Even Benyst nodded his approval.

"So the outfit is a success," I said, "let's hope everything else goes as well as the fashion."

"Well, let's find out," Royal said as he opened the front door.

We stepped out onto the lawn; the sky was a dark blue with a light pink edge growing in the eastern sky. Gathered there in the cool morning mist, we went over the plan. Benyst, Noiryn, Royal, Spin and I would head out. Grog and Brog would stay behind and keep watch. That way we would know if Sid tried to get back through the gate. It was a sound plan.

I led the group to the Travelling area.

"It'll be all right," Royal was bringing up the rear. His voice filled our little area of the forest.

"It has to be," Benyst said.

"That's reassuring," I said.

"He doesn't mean it," Noiryn added.

"Yes, I do," Benyst went on. "This has to work. We must get the minions here, and Phoenix must take a seat on the Guard. If not, the minions will no doubt slaughter each other completely disrupting the power balance of the Void. We must succeed."

"I hadn't thought of that," I mumbled.

I pulled off my gloves and touched my palm. Somewhere in my heart I knew that Rogmesh had received my message.

We were coming.

40

───────

We landed just outside the entrance to the Caves. It was nighttime, like always. The torches and cauldron were lit once more, basting the opening in an undulating light. Rogmesh was there to meet us.

"Phoenix! It is good to see you again so soon," he smiled, revealing a set of very brown and slightly broken teeth. At that moment I realised I'd never noticed minion teeth before. I wondered if all minions had gross teeth. I glanced at Spin, but his mouth was closed. Then I scolded myself for not keeping my head in the game.

"Rogmesh, we have a lot to talk about."

"Come take your throne, and we shall discuss it."

"No, I need to fill you in out here."

I told him what Sid had said. He gasped, and again I was distracted by his teeth. Stop judging, Phoenix! But they're gross. Get over it! Okay. As part of my brain talked to itself, the central part explained our plan to Rogmesh. I intro-duced Benyst and Noiryn and instructed Rogmesh that Spin would be in charge of the settlement and they would work together to run it.

"How do you feel about all this, Rogmesh?"

"Cautiously optimistic. We have been in this dank place for some time, and it will be nice to get some fresh air. I hope that war does not come to us. Those who will go with you are not the most skilled in combat."

"Hopefully it won't come to that."

"And what shall we do with the prisoners?"

"Leave them."

"But who will care for them, bring them food?"

"Oh, right," I paused.

"Leave enough food for three days. After that they are Sid's problem," Benyst said. Rogmesh looked at me.

"What he said."

"It shall be done," Rogmesh answered.

"Please call the minions, I would like to speak to them."

"Of course."

Rogmesh walked over to the entrance to the Caves and held up his hands. In the flickering light of the cauldron, it was hard to see what he was doing. After a few moments, his hands dropped to his sides, and he turned and made his way back to us.

"They are on their way."

A deep rumbling sound rolled up the tunnel and out into grounds before the Caves. The sound had a feeling of weight, and it wrapped around me, hugging me, supporting me, giving me energy and waking my power. I stood there and basked in it as several hundred minions exited the Caves and gathered before me.

"Minions!" my voice came from me easily and yet filled the canyon. "A great threat has been made against us. The one you call Sid has sworn war against me. Soon he will come here and lay claim to the Caves and any minions that remain. Therefore, we must take shelter. I have come to bring you to my home. There we will create a safe place for you to live until the conflict is over. My friends, Benyst and Noiryn, will take you to my home via the Time Tunnel. There, Spin will guide you in creating your shelter." I looked at the minions. They had looked frightened when I told them about Sid, but most visibly relaxed at the thought of leaving. Some still looked unconvinced. "If you wish to stay and join Sid, I will not stop you."

The silence stretched out in front of me.

"What say you, minions?" Rogmesh bellowed at the crowd, and the minions responded.

"We will go with you!"

"Thank you, Phoenix!"

"We must hurry, we must hurry!"

"Quiet!" Rogmesh yelled, and they shut up immediately. Even the peaceful minions could be bossy. "Gather all that you need from the Caves and return at once. You three," he pointed at a cluster of minions, "arrange food for the prisoners. Leave three days' worth by their cells." He pointed at another group of minions. "And you three will guard them in their task." The minions nodded and took off back into the tunnels.

"You're great at this," I said to Rogmesh once the crowd had dispersed.

"Thank you, Phoenix."

"We will make an impressive team," Spin said as he joined us.

"We will," Rogmesh said.

"Bitchin'," I added.

"Phoenix, we have things under control here," Spin smiled. "You and Royal should get going."

"Yes," Benyst said, "I will take the first group."

"I'll get the next one organized," Noiryn said.

"And I will help you," Rogmesh said.

"I will Travel with Benyst," Spin said. "Rogmesh, I shall see you soon."

"Yes, brother."

The group dispersed, leaving Royal and me alone before the cauldron.

"That happened fast," I mumbled. Royal moved in beside me.

"We should get going, girl."

"I'm scared," I whispered.

"Good."

"Good?"

"You should be. This is some serious shit."

"Royal," I couldn't help but laugh, "I've never heard you swear."

"I save it for the important shit," he winked.

"Am I going to get through this?" I asked.

Royal looked at me for a long time. His face was grim, his mouth a hard line. His wings flapped slowly, once.

"Maybe."

41

———

We landed in the Void. I couldn't tell you where because it all looks the same. The land also moves and changes of its own volition, so you never really know where you will land. You just get to the Void and then think hard about where you'd like to be. And hopefully, the Void will comply.

Royal was standing cool as a cucumber beside me. He was an exceptional person to Travel with, super powerful, although he tried to keep that to himself, and he knew how to use his wings as rudders so he could control how he moved along the wave of Time. I watched him sway with the currents and tried to emulate him as best I could. It would take a while to get as smooth as him.

"How you doing, honey?" his voice was unusually quiet.

"I'm good, you all right?"

"Peachy."

"You don't look peachy."

He didn't. His usually tanned and ruddy face had greyed significantly, and his relaxed stance felt forced.

"Well, it's been a while."

"Since you've been in the Void?" He nodded. "How long?"

"Oh, who keeps track? But long enough that everyone forgot I existed." He was trying to be affable, to stop the fear from creeping into his voice, but I could hear it.

"Are you up for this?" Before he could answer, I continued, "Because it's okay if you're not. Talking to the Guard isn't easy, and as much as I'd like you by my side, it's cool if you can't be. I just ask that you wait here for me."

"Phoenix," he took a deep breath, his wings rose and fell with the action, "I'm going with you." I opened my mouth to speak, but he cut me off, "Don't ask me again. I'm okay, and I'm coming with you."

"Okay. Good." I turned on my heel and started walking.

The thing with the Void is you never know where anything is. I'd love to have walked straight into the Circle of the Guard, but I had no idea where it was. It had always just appeared to me. So, counting on it making another appearance, I just picked a direction and started walking. Royal fell into step behind me, and we moved along in world's smallest and saddest conga line.

We had walked for a while when a particularly large rise loomed before us; it had grown out of nowhere and would take effort to climb.

"I reckon what we're looking for is on the other side," Royal said, standing beside me as we both took in the giant hill.

"Yep. That's the Void for you, always a step ahead." As if it heard me, which it did, the ground under our feet sloped away forcing Royal and me to climb if we wanted to keep our balance.

"She definitely heard you."

"She? How do you know it's a she?"

"Because things with immense power usually are."

"Makes sense," I grunted as we climbed. "We could fly over," I offered.

"Not with your wings as they are," Royal answered, "and as a general rule I avoid flying in the Void unless absolutely necessary."

"Why?"

"Because we're the only ones that can do it, and that makes people very jealous. And jealous Travellers are dangerous Travellers."

"We're the only ones? Seriously?"

"Have you ever seen anyone else fly?"

"Well, no, but I haven't seen much."

"Take my word for it."

"So nobody can, like, jump really high or something?" I pressed.

"There's no Superman in the Void."

"Holy crap! Is Superman real?"

"No, Phoenix, it was just an expression."

"Oh, okay," I was a bit disappointed, "but there are vampires, right?"

"Vampires?" Royal thought for a moment. "I've never met one, but I hear they're real."

"Cool."

Royal shook his head.

We had finally made it to the top of the hill. I looked down into the valley below and right there in the centre was the Circle of the Guard.

The Circle was a grouping of tightly spaced trees that formed an impenetrable wall around the Guard. The trees here were much taller than others in the Void and rose so high that the centre of the Circle was not visible even from our prime vantage point.

"Damn, I was hoping we could get a look at things," Royal said.

I tried to answer, but my heart was suddenly hammering its way up into my throat. All the horrible things that had happened to me in that circle came flooding back. Royal put a sturdy hand on my shoulder and spun me around to face him. He took both my shoulders in his hands and shook me, hard.

"Phoenix!" More shaking. "Phoenix!" He barked. "You gotta slow your breathing, girl." A gentler shake. "Look in my eyes, honey. Look in my eyes."

It took all the effort I could muster to focus on Royal's face. I could see the bristles of his beard, the wrinkles of his skin. My eyes slowly made their way up his face to his sparkling blue orbs. When our eyes met something clicked deep in my chest, and I felt my heart slow down and return to its natural place in the centre of my chest. My breathing slowed and the tightness in my ribs reduced. Royal's eyes flashed and the centre of my power, deep in my core, flared to life. Blue-green flame rolled through my belly and out into my limbs. I felt my spine straighten and my wings stretch against their velvet wrappings. I took a clean, deep breath and let it out slowly, my words floating on the current.

"Thank you."

"You're welcome," Royal let go of me. "I thought you were going to go over the edge on me."

"Just a touch of PTSD. The last few times I was here, sucked."

"I get that."

We stood in silence for a few minutes, both of us

breathing deeply and evenly, almost in protest of what lay ahead.

"Well," I broke the silence, "we'd better get going."

"After you, honey."

We headed down into the valley.

42

"**P**ut your hood up," Royal whispered.

"Excellent idea."

I scooped up the velvet cowl and pulled it down over my face to create a shadow deep enough to hide my healing skin and tufts of hair.

We were standing in front of the Circle's trees; their shiny grey leaves and silver trunks creating a veil between the Guard and us.

"How do I look?"

Royal adjusted my hood and nodded.

"Good."

"Let's do this," I turned to the trees. "Are you going to let us in or what?"

"Classy," Royal grumbled.

But his disapproving sound was soon drowned out by a great aching moan as the trees in front of us bent. The leaves rattled against each other as their silver trunks strained. Soon an opening just wide enough for us to squeeze through appeared.

"That's on purpose," Royal whispered.

"We'll have to fold up to get through."

"And they know it." I glanced at Royal, his jaw was set in a grim smile.

"Here we go."

"I'm right behind you."

I stepped through the trees.

The magic of the Void is infinite. Although we stepped through a thin band of trees, it felt like stepping into another world. Whereas the Void itself was cold and overcast, here on the other side of the trees, the sky was still grey but glowed, bathing the inner circle with a strange bright light. My sensitive eyes blinked hard against it, my thin eyelids doing very little to protect me. Royal gently touched my elbow, I nodded that I was okay and then stepped forward, forcing myself to raise my head and face the group before me.

The Guard.

They were sitting just as I remembered them and the initial shock of it rocked me, and I swayed. Royal grunted, and I shook my head, I was all right. I needed to be all right. I had to be all right.

Cosima sat on the far left dais, her chair a broad leather number with low arms. An upgrade from the one I destroyed the last time I had been in this Circle. On that occasion, it had just been her, her lackey Baba Yaga, who was once again lurking behind Cosima's dais, and Greldrom. They had attacked, I'd fought back. Then I'd had a power flare that had sent them running and destroyed all the towers and chairs in the circle.

Cosima looked at me, and an evil cat-who-ate-the-canary style grin spread across her nasty face. Whereas Noiryn was love and light, this siren was a real stone-cold bitch. She had an ample and curvaceous body, covered in red scales, and her third eye was as black as midnight as it bored into me. Cosima sat back in her chair; apparently, she was saving the spikes that ran down her spine for later. Great.

Next to Cosima sat Mastyx. His mouth stretched into a smile, and his tongue flicked out twice. On the ground, entwined around the base of the dais, were two of his snake boys. I had no idea if it was the same two I'd met during my first forays into the Void, but it didn't really matter. I got the impression that Mastyx had a rotating group of snake-boys that showed up to do his bidding.

Silverwood sat next to Mastyx, his tall tree trunk-like body bent awkwardly into his chair. Why didn't they just get him one that worked for him? Or maybe he was way more comfortable than he looked, who knows. Long branches reached from his head and stretched into the grey sky above, their leaves shimmering in the slight breeze. The last time I had seen Silverwood he had helped me Travel from the jungle. The goal of that trip had been to find Archer, but I'd ended up in the silver dudes' stronghold and in the arms of Mhyr. Good times. Silverwood sat forward in his chair as I approached; the creaking in his trunk was audible even from the other side of the Circle.

Wendiga did not move. He was the member of the Guard I knew the least about, other than he was Yeren's leader. And Yeren had proved to be a disaster of a friend. Oh crap, I still had to go back to my human apartment and clean up that goo she'd thrown around. The bitch had melted my tv trying to capture me. I hope no humans try to get in there before I can do something about it. I tore myself away from my ever-growing to-do list and back to Wendiga.

He sat like a king; strong and impassive. The armour on

his chest and shoulders shone in the indirect light of the Void. He looked proud and, dare I hope, fair.

The next chair was empty. It had been Big G's. Part of me wanted to strut straight towards it and sit down like I owned the place. Part of me knew that would be suicide. Cosima would most definitely lose her mind and attack me, Silverwood and Wendiga would see it as an insult, and Mastyx would probably laugh and call me 'interesting' again.

The only person who would defend me couldn't. He sat at the end of the row. The Archer. My Archer. He looked as devastatingly handsome as ever. Sat in his low-slung concrete chair, the grey light of the Void played beautifully over the silver sheen of his skin, making every contour, every muscle pop. Even with everything at stake here in the Circle, I wanted to lick his broad chest and turn that chair into a playground. Sorry, it's been a while. But I need more skin before anything good can happen. Which is gross if you think about it.

Don't think about it.

They all sat on their respective thrones and watched me make the lengthy walk from the circle of trees to the centre of the Guard. I could see their every move from deep within my hood. Royal kept close and to the right behind me. I knew that his head would be held high and his gait would be relaxed and rolling. Royal knew himself, that was clear, and he didn't give a crap what these Travellers thought of him.

I walked to the middle of the semi-circle of chairs and stood my ground. I made a point of turning to look at each member. When I looked at Archer, his facial expression did not change. He made no movement of recognition. A twinge went through my heart, which my rational mind quickly quieted. We had a secret to keep; we had roles to play. He was playing his perfectly, and I would do the same. I turned away and stared straight ahead, at Silverwood, the unspoken leader of the Guard, and waited.

The silence stretched on for several minutes. Still, I did not speak. I could just make out in my peripheral vision Cosima fidgeting. Good. Still, I did not speak. Finally, after what seemed an eternity, Silverwood broke the silence.

"Welcome, Phoenix."

It was like a spell had broken; Cosima chattered about my presence there, Baba Yaga slipped out of sight, the snake boys at Mastyx's feet started slithering around his dais, Mastyx shouted at Cosima to calm down. Even Wendiga started talking, albeit more quietly, questioning Silverwood's greeting to me. The only members of the Guard who remained still and silent were Silverwood and Archer.

Using the cacophony as cover, Royal whispered to me: "Take off your hood."

I reached up with my velvet-clad hand and, stretching my wings wide as I did so, gently pulled back my hood.

43

———

The effect was instantaneous. Even though I was more healed than ever, I was still a shocking site, an extreme visual. I didn't think it was possible for Cosima to shut up as completely as she did, but she was immediately silent and staring. Mastyx had already seen my face, but he too was silenced by the unveiling.

Silverwood slumped back sharply into his chair, a loud crack sounding as he did so. Wendiga silently turned his head from side to side, trying to figure out what had happened to me. Archer shifted in his chair. I glanced over at him and saw a single pewter tear slip from his eye. He wiped it away. His reaction was touching and made me want to hold him.

"What happened to you?" Wendiga's grim bass tones swept through the circle.

"I Burned," I stood there and let the words sink in.

"But why?" Wendiga pressed. Royal made a small coughing sound behind me as if to say 'don't say too much.'

"It is one of the many defence mechanisms my people possess."

"Yes, and here's another question," this was from Mastyx now, "who the hell is he? I thought there was only one of you."

Mastyx is an outstanding actor. He had seen Royal back in the forest near my home, but from his words now you would never have guessed.

"The name's Royal," Royal said as he stepped forward. "And as far as there being only one of us, well, did you ever bothered to check?"

"I thought you were dead," Silverwood's voice was a dry whisper.

"Nope," Royal answered, but for a moment I thought Silverwood had directed his comment at me.

"I have come to take my place on the Guard." My words echoed through the Circle.

"I'm not done talking about your face!" Cosima cackled. "Does the rest of you look like a plucked chicken too?" She continued in a mocking tone, her third eye staring directly at my crotch. "Do you look like that everywhere?"

"Grow up, Cosima," I quipped. "I have bested the one called Greldrom and lay claim to his seat. I have come here to take my place on the Guard."

"You cannot be serious," Wendiga said. "Yes, a new member arrives when an old one dies or takes the throne by killing the current member, but you are not in such a position. You are not a minion. You cannot kill Greldrom and take his seat. It doesn't work like that."

"And why can't it?" Silverwood asked, a faraway look on his face. "If the minions follow her, is she not their leader?"

"They follow me," I said, I needed to get this sewed up before Sid turned up. "They do. In fact, I have convinced them to leave the City of Caves and start a new settlement near my home."

"They left the Caves?" Cosima asked, looking confused by this fresh information.

"Yes, and they were happy to do it. I am now their leader."

"Prove it," Cosima hissed.

"Shut it, Cosima," Mastyx snapped. "If the minions follow her, why shouldn't she be their representative?"

Cosima leapt forward to the edge of his dais and hissed at Mastyx, who immediately hissed back. Two sets of fangs glinted in the grey light of the Void.

"Enough!" Silverwood shouted, the two relaxed back into their respective seats. "We should allow Phoenix to join the Guard."

"But it cannot be so simple!" Wendiga bellowed. "Never in the history of the Void have we allowed cross-species representation. We cannot start now, not without the approval of all creatures."

"Then why don't we get it?" It was the first time Archer had spoken. He was a man of few words and when he spoke the Guard listened.

"And how do you suggest we do that?" Wendiga asked.

"I leave that to my esteemed colleagues," Archer said with a wave of his hand.

"Let me think a moment." Silverwood sat forward in his chair and bowed his head, deep in thought. I snuck a glance at Royal, who smiled when I caught his eye.

"Oh!" Cosima squealed. "I've got it! A Challenge! She should have to go to every species' council and fight their best warrior. If she wins every match, then she can join the Guard."

"That's ridiculoussssssss," Mastyx hissed.

"No, it's not! Greldrom must be avenged!"

"Oh please, Cosima, you were never his friend. You just

liked his violent streak. And what you propose is far too dangerous an endeavour."

"Wait," Silverwood interjected before Cosima could respond, "perhaps not."

"You cannot be serious?" Wendiga said, outrage plain in his voice. "We cannot send her to battle every council in the Void."

"No, you are right," Silverwood agreed. "Not a battle then, perhaps simply a trial. Death not guaranteed. Let each council decide how they wish to test the mettle of this Traveller. Let them determine how they wish to determine her worthiness to join the Guard."

"That sounds fair," Cosima grinned broadly. "Archer's people will tear her apart."

"Death is not guaranteed," Silverwood affirmed.

"Fine, they'll still mess her up," Cosima smiled.

"What say you, Archer?" Wendiga asked.

My stomach dropped as all eyes turned to Archer.

This was getting out of hand. They were about to tell me to go fight everyone in the Void. Okay, not everyone, but an individual from each species. I really didn't think I'd survive that, despite Silverwood's assurances that death was not guaranteed. I tried not to show any fear as I looked at Archer. How the hell would he get me out of this? I wracked my brain and couldn't think of a single reason Archer would have for disagreeing with the others. His approval of this trial challenge thing was almost a done deal. I felt something brush my hand and started, but it was only Royal standing close by my side. A silent show of support.

"I'm here," he whispered. Okay, not so silent.

Archer did not move, not a muscle. He looked relaxed and at ease as he sat in that low-slung chair with my fate in his hands. When he spoke his voice caught in his throat for the briefest of moments, the only betrayal of his actual emotions.

"I think it is a sound plan."

"Then it's settled!" Cosima clapped her hands. "She will face the species' Councils!"

"Calm yourself," Wendiga bellowed, "we must take an official vote."

"All those in favour?" Silverwood asked.

"Now hang on," Mastyx interrupted, "exactly what are we in favour of?" If I didn't know any better, I'd say he looked a little scared.

"We are voting to send Phoenix to the Council of every species of the Void. There she will face a trial of their choosing."

"And will she be allowed help on this journey?" Mastyx asked.

Silverwood pondered the question.

"She may take a group of six individuals with her, one for every council she will face. Her entourage may assist her in a manner agreed upon at the time by the parties involved. And she must complete these trails by the rising of the next full moon." Silverwood turned to Mastyx. "Satisfied?"

"Yesssss," Mastyx mumbled.

"Then I ask again, all those in favour?" Silverwood extended his arm; sitting in the palm of his hand was a compact ball of green light. It left his palm and floated to a spot just above my head.

Cosima's ball was next; it practically shot across the circle. Wendiga and Archer's balls followed. Mastyx was the last to cast his ball of light; it took its time crossing the circle and hovered a few inches away from the others.

"It is done," Silverwood declared.

"So now what?" I asked. I was trying to find a feeling of outrage, but it was buried under a lot of fear.

"Now you must go to the Councils and take the Trials," Wendiga said.

"But who are these Councils? Where are they? How will they know I'm coming?" I was freaking out. I had an impending minion war on my hands. Now I had to pass a bunch of crazy Traveller Trials before the next full moon? Shit just got more serious than usual.

"As their representatives on the Guard, we will each send word of your imminent arrival," Wendiga continued. "You must complete these Trials as quickly as possible, do not dawdle."

Dawdle? What decade are we in? Oh wait, we're not in a decade. Right.

"Okay, but again, who are they and where do they live?"

"There are Archer's people, the silver men," Mastyx jumped in and started giving me the details. "Then the yetis, like Wendiga. There are also the sirens and the trees."

"Don't forget the Pain People!" Cosima interjected. "They get a vote here but never come to meetings. Conflict makes them ugly, and they are so very vain," she laughed.

"Pain People?" I whispered to Royal.

"Like Benyst," he whispered back.

"Ohhhhh."

"And then us," Mastyx continued, "the snake men. We'll have an excellent time together."

"No, Mastyx!" Silverwood shouted. "The councils must handle the challenges, we cannot get involved!" The yelling was very out of character for him. His leaves were shaking.

"Of course, Silverwood. I will not interfere," Mastyx cooed, a sly look on his scale-covered face.

"That's great and all, but how do I find them?" I strung

the words out slowly, I was getting pissed off. Hey, it was better than scared.

"Instructions will be sent to you," Silverwood sat back in his chair like the matter was closed. "You may leave."

Apparently, it was.

"What happens if she doesn't win these Trials?" Royal asked.

"Shit, I hadn't thought of that," I whispered to him.

"If she fails," Silverwood answered, "then she will most likely be dead."

"Okay," I said, "good to know."

I turned to Royal, who nodded, and we walked out the way we came.

44

———

Royal and I exited the Circle of the Guard with no problems. Which was super weird for me since I'd never had the pleasure of being in the Circle without a problem, let alone just walking out. As soon as we crossed through the trees, I turned to Royal to strategize. Before I could open my mouth, he held up his hand and shook his head, making that zipped lip gesture which apparently is as universal as the sign for choking. I got the message, and we walked back to the Travel point, the Void now providing us with smooth level ground, without talking.

We landed back in my forest to the sounds of a commotion. Minion screams and loud bangs reached our ears. In the distance, I could see white smoke rising from the campsite area. I was running before Royal could stop me.

"Phoenix, stop! It could be a trap!"

Yeah, it could be, it probably was, but I sure as hell wasn't going to let shit go down on my proverbial front porch. I ran along the forest path, my wings aching to support my weight and make quick work of this journey.

The screams were getting louder.

I rounded a bend in the path and the clearing stretched out before me. The minions were under attack. By other minions. I couldn't see Sid, he was probably acting as puppet master. It was a blitz attack. That was clear from the craters that were still smoking. I ran through the haze towards the centre of the clearing, where I knew Spin had set up his camp. Minions were running everywhere, I grabbed one as it passed by and it screamed a long ragged sound before it saw my face. Then it went silent.

"What happened?" I asked as tears welled up in its eyes.

"They came out of nowhere!" it cried. "They started throwing bombs and everything was smoking! I couldn't see! I can't find my family! Please help me!"

"That's exactly what I'm going to do." I gave the little minion a reassuring grip on the arm. "I just need to find my friend."

At that moment Royal appeared. He moved through the smoke like an avenging angel, his wings opening and closing, fanning the smoke away. He saw me and was at my side in a moment.

"The bad guys attacked, eh?"

"Yep. Can you get this minion inside the gate? And then round up all the ones on our side and get them inside too?"

"I can if you give me the authorization to do that."

"What?" It was hard to make out his words through the noise and we were losing time.

"You need to give me permission to let people in!" Royal bellowed above the din.

"Oh! Right!" I bellowed back. "I give you permission!" Something clicked between us. A flash of light went through my mind as a spark passed behind Royal's eyes. We were now connected on a power level. Cool. But there was no time to dwell on it. We had to keep moving.

"Just double check the little guys as they go through. We don't want a bad one bombing us from the inside."

"Got it!" Royal scooped up the minion beside me and disappeared into the smoke.

I watched Royal go, pausing momentarily to scoop up another minion as he ran towards the gate. I turned my attention back to the foggy scene before me.

I could make out tents and fire pits. It looked like Spin had gotten everyone set up in a kind of grid formation leading out from his camp. I moved forward slowly, trusting my black jumpsuit would hide me in the swirling drifts of pure white smoke. I felt a tingling down my spine and pulled my sword from its sheath at my back. The sword glowed faintly blue in the indirect light. I kept moving.

Although I could hear minions yelling and screaming, no more minions crossed my path. I thought I saw one run by in the distance, but I couldn't be sure. They must be in hiding. I was torn, I wanted to shout out and let them know Royal was at the gate to help them, but I didn't want to set them up for slaughter in the smokey shadows near the gate. So I kept walking forward, my sword ready.

I reached Spin's camp site. His tent was torn from its posts and pooled on the ground. I used the tip of my sword to lift the fabric and make sure he wasn't inside uncon-scious. It was empty. His fire had burned down to red coals and greying ash, the remnants of a roasted squirrel, tossed carelessly into the pit. I got down low and tried to look under the smoke. From this vantage point, I could see little minion hands and feet moving around about fifteen feet away. One of these minions dropped low and for a moment we were face to face across the clearing. I kept my face neutral, unsure if they were friend or foe. The minion in question snarled and disappeared into the smoke.

"Foe, it is," I whispered to myself.

"Phoenix!" came a hushed whisper behind me. I turned on my heel as the sound of little feet patted quickly toward me. "Thank the gods, you're back!" Spin looked terrible. He had a gash above his left eye and a split lip. He also had a growing bruise on his chest and his loincloth was torn.

"Are you okay?" I asked.

"I'll be fine."

"What happened?"

"They came, the bad ones came and attacked us while we ate!"

"Where are the others?"

"Everyone scattered, I tried to keep order, but they were too frightened." Tears welled up in his big brown eyes.

"It's okay, Spin. We're going to get through this," I patted him on the shoulder and wrapped his arms around me. I gave him as tight a hug as I dared with his injuries, then he pulled away. "Royal is at the gate, I have authorized him to let our minions in. I need you to gather all the minions you can find and send them to the gate. Everyone will be safe once they're inside."

"But what about the bad ones?"

"I'll take care of them," I lifted my sword, Spin's eyes widened. "Big G style if need be. Now go find your friends."

"Yes, my lady."

He bowed quickly and disappeared into the smoke.

45

I stayed down low; the smoke was lighter here and I could see out into the campgrounds. Most of the tents were destroyed, which limited the cover available.

"You bastards can't hide forever," I whispered into the smoke.

I heard the quick patter of steps off to my right and spun towards it just in time to see a minion with a short blade running full-tilt towards me. I had a split second to decide what to do. If I stood up for a better strike, I would lose my visual on this jerk-off. So I stayed low and got one foot under me for leverage. The minion continued to charge, but at the last second dashed off to the left into the smoke. I had just enough time to go 'what the hell?' when I felt something slam into the back of me. Another minion. Fortunately, this guy didn't have a blade, just a small club which he brought repeatedly down on my head. I jumped to my feet and swung my sword up and back over my head and felt the blade slice down the back of the offending minion. It screamed and fell to the ground. A sharp cry sounded and new a minion rolled into my legs, knocking them out from under me.

I landed on my back and felt my delicate wings crack underneath my weight. I screamed with the pain and swung my sword erratically around me. It clipped something, but that didn't stop a third minion, the one with the blade, from joining in the fun.

Tiny stabs started up my legs. I kicked out and felt my foot connect with minion skull. I threw an elbow at the minion who was still clubbing my head and freed myself long enough to get to my feet. Standing was better for fighting, but now I had lost my view of the ground. I kept swinging my sword, sometimes I made contact with my attackers, sometimes I didn't. The minions could be anywhere.

Anywhere turned out to be everywhere.

I could just make out in the swirling smoke a great mass of minions heading towards me. It was like the City in the Trees all over again.

"Damn it, boys, we've done this before," I grunted.

The minions closed in; I kept slicing. Now every move of my blade met with minion flesh. If I had thought to end this diplomatically, I was sorely mistaken. These guys were out for my blood and I would not give it to them.

I felt a blade hit my lower back and my legs buckled. As I went down the minions flowed over me like a wave. There were so many hands, so many blades and teeth biting at my skin. I had been here before too many times. In the past, it had frightened me, but now I had been to the other side. Now I knew what it was to Burn, and no creature would ever send me to that place again.

I took a deep breath and let it out slowly. Then another. My attackers continued their onslaught, but I paid it no mind. I focused on the core of power deep in the centre of my body, and I called it forth. It came screaming to the surface of my skin and poured bright white light from every cut, slit and tear of my suit. I felt the minions recoil from the light and I rushed to my feet. Blinded by my power, the minions were easy pickings. My blade slashed and soon the ground was covered in the multicoloured beauty of minion blood.

Then everything was quiet.

I stood in a pile of minions. There were many bodies, but not as many as I knew we'd locked in the cells. There were more bad guys out there.

The smoke had lifted; the retreating grey mist exposing the extent of the attack. As I gazed upon the battlefield, my skin started to itch: first up my legs and along my arms, then through the thickness of my torso. Even my face itched. I felt like a snake that needed to shed its skin. I ran my gloved hands over my body, but it did little to relieve the itching and only made my wounds ooze.

Suddenly my wings spasmed. The action shot me two feet into the air. I landed hard on a patch of minion blood and fell to the ground. The minion blood quickly seeped into my many cuts, causing a burning sensation in the wounds. I pulled off my gloves and attempted to cut at my pant leg with my sword. My wings spasmed again, and I accidentally drove the tip of my blade deep into my calf.

As the blade bit into my flesh, power shot through me from head to toe and I cried out. My wings flapped uncontrollably. I was bucking all over the ground as they tried to lift me to sky. More minion blood got in my wounds as I thrashed and the itching sensation doubled. I had to get out of these clothes or I was going to Burn myself up.

I tossed my sword to the ground and tore at the fabric

covering my arms and legs with my bare hands, revealing the skin. Where the minion blood had touched my wounds they looked infected, pustules and green ooze covered my thin skin. My wings sensed the dangerous pathogens and dragged me to my feet. I grabbed my sword as I left the ground and slid it down my back, using the edge of the blade to split my suit. The puss and minion blood made the cloth stick to my skin. I pulled it free with my bony fingers, feeling the thin skin of my back tear. I turned my blade to my wings and sliced through the fabric there, freeing them. Under the black velvet cloth were small feathers.

My wings had feathers again.

I had feathers again.

I stood there naked, covered in puss, and as I looked at those feathers, my heart soared. Bright blue power flared through my torso, visible through the thin skin stretched over my ribs. It moved through my body, forcing the minion blood from my limbs. I watched as the poison and puss streamed down my body to the ground at my feet.

My wings stretched out to their full width as the bright blue light filled them with power. Before my very eyes, I saw the feathers grow fully formed. My wings flapped, gracefully, elegantly, like they had never been less than they were right now. They pulled me into the sky and as the air caressed my naked skin; I felt my many wounds heal. I felt my skin thicken. I felt my muscles grow.

I could see the shimmering dome of power that protected my lands. My wings took me home. I passed through the wall of power and felt the last bits of decay leave my heart and mind. I felt my body return from its grim journey, whole, strong, and ready to kick major ass.

I landed on the vast lawn of my home. A strand of long

dark hair fell in front of my eyes and I swept it aside with an elegant hand. I stood there naked, whole and glorious.

Everyone stared.

The minions dropped to their knees.

"I'm back, bitches."

THE END

CONTINUE THE ADVENTURE...
Rise
The Phoenix Series Book 4
Available Now!

THE STORY DOESN'T END HERE

The story doesn't end here.

If this book stirred something in you—

if you want more of the strange, the cinematic, or the stories that meet you where the shadows are deepest—

you're in the right place.

When you sign up for my mailing list, you'll get early access to new releases, behind-the-scenes lore, letters from my strange and unusual world, and first word when new episodes of my podcast *We Make Art* go live.

Sign up and join me on this adventure:

https://sarahrockwood.com/mailing-list/

SPREAD THE WORD

If this book moved you, let it move others too.

Reviews are powerful. They help stories like this find their way into the right hands—and into the quiet hearts that need them most.

If you enjoyed what you just read, consider leaving a review on your favourite book-loving platform and the store where you picked it up. Even a few words can make a difference.

And if it stirred something worth sharing, tell your people. Whisper it, post it, pass it on.

You're part of how this story travels.
Thank you.

RISE

Everyone stared at me. In the hazy smoke that drifted in from the battlefield just outside my gates, I could see them, their shadowy forms, as they looked at me. On their knees in supplication, the minions gazed up from where they crouched to take in my glory.

My wings had returned to me. They were a magnificent sight stretching out from my back. The colours in the feathers had become richer, deeper, but no less vibrant. I was a glorious parrot on steroids. I stretched the wings in and out, my feet lifting gently from the ground. I could live forever barely touching the soil.

My sword was still at my back, its smooth leather sheath against my naked flesh. I reached for the hilt, and my hair parted magically around it. I gently caressed the handle but left the sword where it was. I was on my lands. There was no need for it here. My hair swirled again to cover the blade.

My hair was longer than ever, it grazed my naked ass as its bulk swirled behind me, caught in a draft that seemed to emanate from my very self. I felt taller, but that was probably just the freshness of my spine. The new bones and sinews singing with excitement as they moved together.

I looked down at my body, my skin was perfect: no blemishes, marks or scars. I delicately touched my face; it was smooth and whole, and over each eye was a thick brow. Reaching into my mouth, I felt my teeth with my fingers. The permanent retainer thing I'd had since I was fourteen was gone, as were my crowns. I now had however many teeth you're supposed to have, sitting pretty in my mouth.

I was perfect. I was whole. I was a rock star.

I looked at the crowd. No one made a sound. After the noise of the battle, it unnerved me.

"Isn't anyone going to say anything?" I called out. "I've just done some serious metamorphic shit over here. No one has a comment?"

I could see Noiryn and Benyst by the great doors to my home. Noiryn clung to Benyst like she'd seen a ghost, her third eye racing up and down my body. Benyst's mouth stretched into a tight, thin line. I caught movement in my periphery and spun towards it. The minions gasped. Had it been that fast? I felt a little quicker on my feet than usual, but nothing crazy.

My eyes locked on the creature that had moved and I realised it was Spin. He wore a bloodstained apron and held a dark cloth in his hands.

"Spin!" I started walking towards him, the minions parting before me like a wave. "What do you think?" I gestured at my perfectness, "Pretty great, eh?"

"Yes, my lady," he bowed. Up close, I could see the fine lines etched around his eyes. "I wonder though, are you all right?"

"What?" I shook my head, my luxurious hair swinging

around me. "Of course I'm all right. Look at me!" Spin flinched. Was my voice a bit too loud?

"Yes, your beauty is obvious," he smiled. "It just happened so quickly, I wonder if you are okay? If the transition was not too difficult?"

I didn't like the look on his face; it looked like pity. The last thing I needed was pity from some grey minion when I looked like a supermodel.

"Are you okay?" he asked quietly.

"I'm better than okay," I blurted. "I'm disappointed in you, Spin. I thought you of all people could see that."

I spun on my heel and left him there with that weird look on his face.

As I crossed the lawn towards the doors to my home, Noiryn and Benyst stepped aside, Benyst gently pressing Noiryn behind him. I scowled.

"You don't need to do that, Benyst. I'm not going to hurt her."

"You seem edgier than usual; you know she doesn't like that," Benyst practically growled.

"Wow, well maybe 'she' can speak up for herself?" I looked at Noiryn, "are you going to say something?"

"Phoenix, why are you shouting?" she whispered.

"Are you kidding me?" I laughed, "Look at me! I fixed myself, completely fixed myself, I look fucking glorious and obliterated a bunch of bad minions by the way, and everyone is looking at me like I've lost my mind!" I laughed again. It felt like hard bubbles in my chest. "What is wrong with you people?"

"Hey, honey," a soft, gravelly voice reached my ears. Royal had stepped out onto the front steps. "How about you go put some clothes on?" he smirked, "Your gloriousness is a bit too much for us all right now."

"Fine."

I brushed past Benyst and Noiryn, then, without think-ing, I flew to the top of the stairs. I gasped and looked back at Royal, but it was too dark in the entryway to see his face.

- 2 -

I threw open the door to my room, tossed my sword on the bed and went straight to the wall of mirrors that were my closets.

I was beautiful. More beautiful than I had ever been in my life.

I posed before the glass, turning side to side, stretching out my wings to get the best angle to admire myself. My hair moved on its own, there was no breeze in the room and yet it undulated and curled around me subtly, always framing my face just so. I gazed at my curves; my breasts were high and firm, and my ass was rounder and prouder than ever. And my legs! They were long and lean and yet supple through the thighs. Here before me, in the bright reflection of the mirror, was my perfect self.

I heard a soft click as the bedroom door closed and saw Grog and Brog at my feet, reflected in the glass.

"Hey, guys! What do you think?"

They said nothing. Brog tottered a bit as he dug his stony claws into the carpet. The chunk of stone missing from his head was more pronounced in his reflection. Grog looked at me in the glass, I watched him take in every inch of my new body.

"You look beautiful, my lady," he breathed.

"Thank you, Grog. You're the first person to say that," I smiled at myself. "Not that I need telling, I look fantastic! It's almost a shame to put clothes on." I winked at the gargoyles.

They didn't move. "Come on, guys! Say something, please. I've just been through this amazing metamorphosis, my body is finally back and better than ever, and everyone is acting like I'm a freak or something."

"It just happened so fast, my lady," Grog said slowly, "It's a lot to take in."

"You don't look right." The words tumbled quickly from Brog's mouth. "Your eyes are too bright. And your face looks funny."

I jerked like he'd slapped me. Usually one could count on Brog for some home-spun truth, a bit of honesty wrapped up in a cuddly stone package, but he was saying some crap right now. I stepped up to the glass and looked closely at my face. It was beautiful, the planes of my cheekbones were high and smooth, the arch of my eyebrows subtle and flattering. My lips were full and lush, curved pleasantly into just the hint of a smile, even when I relaxed my face. Were my eyes too bright? No, they sparkled. The roundness was youthful, and the whites of my eyes had never been whiter. My eyes shone like the fucking star I was. I glanced back and saw that Grog and Brog were still staring. I sighed heavily.

"I look beautiful; I don't need a couple of gargoyles to agree with me." I strutted before the glass, opening all the closet doors as I went. "Brog, you know my clothes, pick something out for me, and Grog, you're good with the accessories, find some stuff that matches. I need to take a shower." I left the ungrateful gargoyles to their work.

Thirty minutes later, I was making my way down the stairs clad in a skin-tight patent-leather, silver jumpsuit with matching boots and sheath for my sword. The suit had long liquid sleeves with little rings that slipped over my middle finger so it covered the back of my hands. A deep V plunged in the front and back, exposing the soft curves of my breasts and joinings of my wings. Sheathed in platinum, my sword stood out again the milky whiteness of my skin as it nestled between my magnificent wings. The shower had washed the last of the battlefield dust from my feathers, and now my wings practically shone in the warm light of the foyer. I let my hair go free; it was still moving gently around me on its own magical breeze. A small part of my mind wondered if that was normal, but the rest of me told it to shut up.

I stood at the top of the stairs like mercury, the element and the rock-star, every eye in the place turned to me. Well, they would have had there been anyone in the foyer.

"Where is everyone?"

"They are out helping the injured, my lady," Grog said. I turned to him and noticed he was alone.

"Hey, where's Brog?"

"He is resting."

"Why?"

"He is tired."

"Why is he tired?" I huffed, "It's not like he does anything."

Grog stared at me for a moment.

"He has been up for many hours helping in the kitchen."

"The kitchen? Why?"

"We have been making food for the minions; there are a great number of them."

"Can't they make their own food?"

"Of course, but every little bit helps."

"Right."

Grog kept staring at me. The obsidian orbs of his eyes didn't move from my face, I could feel them on me even as I glanced around the foyer. It was pissing me off.

"If you've got something to say, Grog, say it."

He took a deep breath and smiled

"No, my lady. If there is nothing else, I will go check on my brother."

"You may go."

Grog nodded to me and padded back along the hallway.

"Oh good, you're dressed," Royal's sardonic twang echoed through the front hall. "You better get out here."

I leapt from the top step and, with my wings spread, landed smoothly in front of him.

"Impressed?" I asked.

"Sure," he chirped and walked back through the massive oak doors.

Rise is available now from your favourite retailer!

ABOUT THE AUTHOR

Sarah Rockwood is a storyteller of the strange and unusual. Her fiction reads like film—visceral, lyrical, and a little bit odd. Tales that invite readers into shadowed worlds where heroines reclaim their power one scene at a time. Her writing and music have appeared in film, television, and bookshelves across the globe.

Raised on a steady diet of *The Muppets*, *David Bowie*, and *The Rocky Horror Picture Show*, her stories are likely to keep you turning pages well past your bedtime.

For more of the strange and unusual, visit: SarahRockwood.com